From Lullabies to Love Songs and Funeral Dirges

Edited by Gregory Roberts-Gassler

ISBN: 9781794068469

To Love and be loved

To Loved Ones and Family

Yours and Mine and Ours

Editor's Preface

When I first found the Everett Creative Writers Group on Meetup, we were meeting at a Panera. It was noisy and sometimes crowded, but the food there was good and the company cheerful. Nowadays, we meet at a fancier place downtown in a private back room, which makes it feel much less crowded, although not necessarily less noisy once they started hiring a Thursday Night musical act. But the noise has never put us out of our mood because as a group, we have always been dedicated to each other's stories.

I, for one, felt welcomed with open arms. Our group is (we now know from experience) not for everyone, but it has been for me. My only frustration in the first few years I was coming was that while we kept coming to the group, few of us were going anywhere else.

This book started off as a way to remedy that. It's a kick in the pants to jump-start all our careers as writers of fiction (and non-) as well as opportunity to casually practice marketing strategies as a group. (Congratulations on being our guinea-pig, reader!) We decided that any anthology worth its salt requires a theme and after a modicum of discussion, we settled on "love" as being just versatile enough to suit our purposes. Because we didn't want to limit ourselves to romantic love: these stories cover not just love between partners, but the love of parents for their children (and back again), the love of country or humanity itself. Half (well, not quite half, but much) of the fun of this process has been in deciding just how broad we are allowed to make it.

But for me, it has also been an excuse to explore craft in a way that I never had before. Editing more or less runs in my family—my mother made a career as one of the most respected editors and translators into English in Brussels (oh, hush, Mutti, of course you were) and I apprenticed as her often more-reluctant-than-not henchman. Then in grad school in particular, getting myself an MFA in Dramatic Writing from SCAD, I developed quite the reputation (deserved or not) as the Grammar Gestapo, as well as an exacting Story Doctor—a reputation I hungrily carried with me to Everett and its writers.

But the caveat I kept in the back of my mind through this whole process was a horror story related to me by my father about an anthology editor so precise, so exacting, that he micromanaged all the flavor out of the stories in his book, pounding his authors' prose into a monochromatic nightmare of repetitions and clichés.

This was the last thing I wanted from our volume. These writers are, I dare say, quite different from each other not just in subject matter, but in style and technique, and far be it from me (far, far indeed) to deprive them of their singularity. So if I have erred at all in this experiment, I hope it has been on the side of the individuals.

As to the order of succession, I have tried to arrange the stories here in a progression that mimics either a larger story or perhaps a human life. Maybe a mix-tape. This was my reasoning:

The first story is a fairy tale. In addition to seeming (though, I hasten to add, deceptively) to be the most childish in structure, this piece actually turned out to encapsulate a great many of the themes that came out of the other works.

The next three are more or less conventional love stories, though each with their very own twists: one about young love, one on love a little bit older, and one about love almost lost to tears.

The two after that are arguably about toxic affairs that would have been better off never embarked upon.

Then came two about the oldest love (and the youngest): the love of parents for children and back again.

And then comes the weird stuff: the orange love, the fantasy-satire love and the love that almost doesn't fit on this type of stage.

Finally, the penultimate tale is an epic quest of the heart through wonder and nostalgia to a place of peace.

The last thing on the list (aptly titled "Last Thing on the List") is a fine flash from a friend from a different group just having fun, and the hope that you find comfort and inspiration in reading the rest.

We hope that you enjoy reading these stories at least one thirteenth as much as we enjoyed writing them.

The Gilded Cage

Christine Gustavson-Udd

Born and raised in Minnetonka, Minnesota, Christine Gustavson-Udd is the mother of an adult daughter and son now living in the Pacific Northwest. She studied art and holds a Masters in Elementary Education. She writes and illustrates children's books, currently available on Amazon for Kindle.

Some treat True Love like it's a fairy tale–but not all fairy tales are about true love. Or, if they are, it's not always the kind of love it looks like.

Long ago, in a forest near a quaint little western European village, there lived a purple bird named Aubergine who had the clearest voice and the most beautiful plumage in all the land. By entertaining humans with her song, Aubergine took care of Grandmother, who was quite elderly and could not go out to find food, and also cared for some of the forest creatures.

"If I needed help, they'd help me. It's the neighborly thing to do," the kind bird always said.

Every day after she checked on Grandmother and her neighbors, she went to the village to sing. It was quite a sight to behold! The beautiful purple bird swooped into the town square, the villagers gathered 'round. Aubergine closed her eyes and took a deep breath. On the exhale, she opened her eyes, straightened up tall, took another breath and performed one of her glorious songs.

"Since I was born, I have lived for corn
And the bounteous health it'll bring
How it keeps me warm through the winter storm
and feeds me all through 'til spring..."

The villagers filled her satchel with crusts of bread, nuts and seeds in appreciation, which she shared with Grandmother and the forest creatures.

The tailor was kind enough to let the bird gather stray threads from the floor of his shop. She brought the threads to Grandmother, who crocheted them into dainty handkerchiefs, which she gave to the wee forest families in need of an extra blanket.

One day, while she was singing in the town square, a stranger rode into the village on a white horse. He was handsome and clothed in the finest velvet and silk.

He must be very wealthy, Aubergine thought, *A prince!*

The crowd of villagers parted. The prince rode his horse right up to Aubergine. She stopped singing. Her eyes grew wide. *Have I done something wrong?* she wondered.

"I know not which is lovelier, your heavenly voice or your plumage that shines like amethyst."

"Thank you, your grace," she said, and shyly hid her face with her wing.

"Accompany me to my castle. We shall have a feast in your honor, at which you will sing."

It would be lovely to be able to provide more food for Grandmother. She would be so pleased and so proud of me! Surely there would be extra to share with all the forest families.

But what would Grandmother do without me while I am away? Perhaps I shouldn't go—I don't know this man!

"I'm sorry, but I cannot leave Grandmother alone. She depends on me for her care and feeding."

The prince saw her reluctance. "You will only be gone one night and then return to your Grandmother with more food than she's ever seen."

The prince had made a generous offer, and Aubergine didn't want to appear ungrateful. "Well, if it is only for one night."

"Splendid! We are off to the castle! Huzzah!" With that, the white stallion reared up on his hind legs, his front hooves dancing in the air. When his hooves returned to the ground, he jumped to a gallop, his rider astride this magnificent mount. "Allons-y! Let's go, bird!"

Grandmother has always said, "a stranger is a friend you haven't met yet"—and he is a prince!

⁂

After they left the village, their pace slowed.

Clip-clop, clip-clop, went the horses' hooves.

Aubergine tried to fill the uncomfortable silence: "I've never traveled this far beyond the village. It's quite lovely."

"Yes, but nary as lovely as you," said the prince.

Aubergine turned away to hide her embarrassment.

Clip-clop, clip-clop.

Aubergine composed herself, then asked, "I've never seen you before, what made you come to the village today?"

"News of your singing voice has spread throughout the countryside. I wished to hear it for myself. Your beauty is a welcome surprise." He beamed at her. Her heart raced.

Those piercing blue eyes! His gold velvet cape and purple satin shirt are so luxurious! That horse—only royalty could afford such a magnificent white stallion. And how he speaks to me—such flattery have I never heard before. He could have any kind of fowl he wants! Why has he taken an interest in me? I'm just an ordinary bird...

Clip-clop, clip-clop.

"It must be exciting to be a prince."

He leaned in and whispered, "I sometimes find it tedious. I have many duties."

"Oh, as do I! I care for Grandmother, and some of the forest creatures, too. Though, I don't mind it, really. They'd do the same for me."

After half a day's ride, they arrived at the castle. The sight was spectacular! Uniformed guards stood at the iron gate. Wolves carved from marble stood watch at the entrance. Gargoyles loomed over the courtyard. In the great halls hung grand tapestries, ferocious bears and wolves stood forever frozen in a pose of attack.

The dining room had a crystal chandelier that hung over a long mahogany table, where luscious fruits, savory vegetables, fresh breads, pies, cakes and cookies lay on silver platters. The humble bird had never seen such decadence!

"Oh! Grandmother will be delighted to have even a small taste!"

"Be seated and partake of this sumptuous repast. After which the maid will show you to the guest suite."

"Oh, thank you! Aren't you staying?"

"No, I have other matters to attend to," said the prince, and turned to leave.

Aubergine ate until she thought she'd burst.

"This way, miss," said the maid. She took her to the guest room.

Her eyes grew wide, "Such luxury as I have never seen before!" A frame of gold filigree formed a halo behind a circular bed that was upholstered in red velvet.

She lay upon the velvety bed and was quickly asleep.

"Ah-roooo! Grrrrr! Ah-roo-rooo!" echoed through the halls of the castle. Aubergine was startled awake. She could see nothing in the darkness. She was concerned, but still relieved to be within the safety of the great castle walls.

Next morning, she awoke facing the gold frame and slowly blinked her eyes. *Oh, I'm facing backwards.* She turned around so she could get out of bed. The gold frame was on that side as well. She looked up and down, turned around again. The frame encircled her completely. *What? Oh dear! This can't be.* She grasped the filigree – it was unyielding. *This is a cage!*

The prince entered the room.

"Why am I confined?" she demanded.

"'Tis for your safety, there are great hungry wolves about, who would devour you. 'Tis not to keep you in but keep them out!"

"I need to get back. Grandmother and the forest creatures depend on me for food."

"'Tis much too stormy to travel today," he said, "surely your people would want you to be safe."

"Of course."

"Tomorrow, then," he said.

I hope Grandmother will be all right for another night. I didn't tell anyone I was leaving—is anyone caring for her in my absence? Perhaps I should start back, brave the storm.

"'Tis time for you to sing for my parents."

Her stomach growled loudly. *I hope there will be a meal afterwards,* she thought, but was too polite to ask. "Well, since I agreed to it already," she said. She stood up, prepared to walk to the throne room. The prince picked up the cage. The bird lost her balance and sat back down on the cushion.

The prince carried the caged bird down the hall to the entrance of the throne room, two huge doors decorated with gold leaf. She grew nervous and the prince smiled at her discomfort. A guard opened the great doors; they proceeded down a long aisle to a man and woman, seated on magnificent thrones covered in gold and jewels. They were dressed in fine velvet and silks and wore crowns of gold encrusted with jewels.

"Mother, Father, may I present to you this unusual bird. I found her singing in the town square, and I thought you'd enjoy hearing her, too."

The bird curtsied. "I'm Aubergine. It's a pleasure to make your acquaintance, your majesties."

"Why have you brought such an insolent creature that addresses the king before he has given her permission to speak?" demanded the king.

Aubergine was unaware of her error. She dropped her head to her breast and trembled with fear.

"She is a gifted singer. I had thought you would enjoy hearing her sing," the prince said, and turned to look at the bird.

Aubergine closed her eyes and took a deep breath. On the exhale, she opened her eyes, straightened up tall, took another breath—

"Well, you are here to sing, so sing!" demanded the red-faced king.

Aubergine started to shake again. Suddenly, the room seemed to be getting smaller, she couldn't get the deep breath she needed. She tried to sing, but her nerves wouldn't allow it. She only managed a squeak and a croak.

The queen looked down her long slender nose at the bird. "Often pretty birds are thought more talented than they actually are."

Aubergine began to cry. "My apologies, your majesties."

The king, with a wave of his hand, said, "Begone!" The prince picked up the caged bird and dashed out of the throne room.

"I should like to return to the forest," Aubergine said through tears.

"'Tis much too dark now. Tomorrow you may go, should the weather permit."

They returned to the guest quarters. "I should like to sleep on the floor, rather than in a cage."

The prince smirked. "Well, if you enjoy being devoured by wolves in your sleep."

"Of course not. The castle walls should keep them out, shouldn't they?"

"Well, they should, although wolves have been known to breach the walls."

Aubergine shifted back and forth, from one foot to the other, her eyes darted around the room. The stone walls looked solid.

"'Tis better to be safe than sorry, is it not?"

"Yes. Grandmother always says, 'Better safe than sorry.' I will sleep in the cage."

"Good, it's settled then."

"Please, may I have some fresh straw from the stables?"

"What ever for?"

"I would like to build a nest."

"You have a velvet bed upon which to sleep. Does it not please you?"

"Oh, it's divine! But I feel the need for a more traditional bed." She hoped she wouldn't need to explain further.

"If that is what you wish. I will have one of the servants bring you some straw."

"Thank you, your majesty."

Aubergine took great care building her nest from the straw and lined it with her soft downy feathers. She was pleased with the nest and settled into a deep sleep, at least for a little while.

That night, she heard the wolves howling and growling again. She was grateful she was in the safety of a cage.

In the morning, the prince came into the guest room and saw that Aubergine had laid three eggs. "Oh, how lovely!" he said and smiled sweetly.

"These eggs should hatch in the forest—our real home."

"Wouldn't you prefer to raise your hatchlings here? You shall want for nothing."

"They'll be more comfortable with their own kind, and I need to get back to Grandmother."

"They belong here." The prince folded his arms across his chest. "I shall decide what is best for them."

"How could a man know what is best for them? I am their mother and a bird!"

The prince opened the cage door.

Aubergine thought he was letting her go, but he reached in and grabbed her by the throat.

"Man hath dominion over beasts and birds! You shall not speak to me that way! Are you ready to apologize?" he asked, still holding on tight.

She couldn't answer. He threw her down onto her eggs. Aubergine gasped, "Oh dear!" She hoped her precious eggs would be all right.

"See what you made me do?" he shouted and slammed the cage door shut and locked it.

Aubergine couldn't understand why the prince was suddenly so cruel. More than ever, she wanted to go home, to get her eggs to safety. "I never should have come to this place," she said quietly.

"Have I not provided you a feast? Have you not slept in luxury fit for a queen?"

"Yes, sire, but I should like to return home; Grandmother and the others need me."

"My castle, 'tis far superior to your hovel!" he shouted, and left.

Aubergine cried until she could cry no more. Then she began quietly singing to her eggs, the songs every mama bird knows. She warmed them, they started to grow, and she grew to love them. She whispered, "Someday soon, little ones, when you are fledglings and your wings are ready for flying, we shall escape this place and return to the forest and to Grandmother, to live out our lives singing and soaring in the sunshine."

She tried to remain optimistic, but Aubergine couldn't help worrying. *Are the woodland creatures caring for Grandmother? Is she worried about me? Has anyone else noticed I'm gone?*

How I wish I'd never left my beautiful forest home with the sweet-smelling pines and the quaint village nearby. The villagers are so kind... I thought all humans would be.

Aubergine sat on her eggs in the cage, day after day. She dared not go out for she feared leaving them alone and unprotected. Daily, the prince came to taunt her. "'Tis a misfortune you have lost your lovely voice. It seems the queen was correct: pretty birds are often told they are more talented than they actually are. They should see you now; your bright feathers have fallen out, the dull ones left behind. They would not think your songs so lovely anymore," he sneered.

I must find a way to escape this hurtful man and this dreadful place, for myself and for my children.

Aubergine figured out how to open the cage, so that when they were ready, they could flee.

The day came when her eggs began to hatch. Aubergine was so happy that from her burst forth a song of jubilation!

"Little chick, little chick,
Welcome to the world!
Little chick, little chick,
How brightly you've unfurled!

Past is dark, but future's long
And always, you'll have friends
To help you if there's something wrong
Or guide you to your ends."

She watched as two perfect hatchlings emerged from the eggs.

Aubergine scrutinized the third egg; she gently rolled it around, hoping to encourage the chick to free itself. That's when she discovered the crack. She froze and choked back her tears.

Aubergine spread her wings, encircling the nest.

"My dearest two little ones, how happy I am you are here, and that you have each other. For just a moment, I'd like to honor your lost sibling." In a somber tone, she sang:

"Little one we never knew,
Although we'll never meet,
Know my love was also for you
And our family will not be complete."

A tear escaped for her lost chick. Turning back to the other two, she sang—

"Still we three will carry on
And still we three will sing!
But from this place we must be gone
Or we'll lose everything!"

She closed in tighter, pulling the chicks to her breast. Her heart was aching, but she didn't want them to be heartbroken, like she, over the lost chick. She wanted them to celebrate each other, and a life full of possibilities.

She was overjoyed that the hatchlings had come, but concerned. She hadn't eaten since the meal upon her arrival—how would she feed hungry baby birds?

The maid heard the songs and gingerly peeked her head into the room. Her eyes grew wide and so did her smile. She was surprised and delighted to see the tiny baby birds.

"I hate to be a bother, but could you please find something I could feed to my hatchlings?" asked Aubergine.

"The master has told the staff to stay out of this room," the maid said, barely above a whisper. She looked over her shoulder, then added, "But I cannot let you starve. I'll find something." And she secretly brought them bugs and worms, which is just what baby birds need to make them grow strong.

After a few weeks, Aubergine thought the chicks were large enough to fly. She asked the maid, "Please open the window so that we may escape this place?"

"No, Miss Aubergine! My master will fly into a rage and dismiss me! My family depends on the money I send them to survive!"

"Then leave a window somewhere else unlocked, and I shall exit there."

The maid thought about it. She looked around to see if they were alone. In a hushed tone, she said, "If you went through the kitchen, the door is most always open during cooking times. Then you could escape, and it would be no one's fault."

Aubergine waited until an hour or so before the midday meal, then she opened the cage and led her fledglings through the great halls. How enormous the halls seemed now she was traveling with two little ones. They hopped and practiced flying in short spurts as they made their way closer to freedom.

Ping-ting-ting! echoed through the halls.

"Sweet chicks, that's enough flight practice for now," Aubergine whispered. "I don't want you to be all tired out before we get outside." She tried not to let them see how

frightened she was, for she knew they could be discovered at any moment.

After what seemed like hours, they reached the kitchen. Aubergine could see the sunshine through the open door. *We're almost free now,* she thought.

Then suddenly, the prince appeared!

He glared at Aubergine. "How dare you try to leave with my chicks!" he shouted.

"Fly, little ones, fly!" she cried out. The chicks flapped their tiny wings and hopped towards the door.

But the prince scooped them up and gave Aubergine a sharp kick out the door, so forceful it sent her end over end, breaking one of her wings. The prince slammed the door shut and locked it. He stood at the window, holding the fledglings.

He opened the window a crack, "Goodbye! 'Tis what you wanted! Go home now!" he sneered. "You have no one to blame but yourself!" He pinched the baby birds, so their mother would hear them squawk. Their cries of pain made her cringe. "Their fate is in my hands now. They will perform for the royal court. If they do not sing to my satisfaction, I will give them to the royal chef," he said with a smirk.

Aubergine was stunned. She'd been so close to escaping! She spread her wings, she had to fly to the window to try to save her babies. She flapped her wings and gasped from the pain, but pain or no, she was determined to fly. She tried getting a running start but couldn't get off the ground. The end of one of her wings hung limp.

The prince saw her struggling and cackled with fiendish delight, "You're damaged goods! You'll never survive without me!" He disappeared from the window with the chicks.

When Aubergine tapped on the door, the chef came, but wouldn't open it. "Please, won't you please let me back in?"

"I cannot, the master says you mustn't be allowed back in."

She went around the side, saw the maid through the window. "Please, won't you let me in?"

"I'm so sorry miss, I cannot."

Aubergine sat down and cried. What was she to do?

She decided to go home. *Surely someone there will help me free my fledglings.*

She walked until nightfall. She couldn't fly to the safety of the tree branches, so she hid under a blanket of leaves. She listened for wolves but didn't hear any. *Strange. The howling was so loud in the castle, it was as though I was surrounded by ferocious wolves...* Though she never saw any, except for the stone statues of wolves at the entry. And she never heard their footsteps— *Wouldn't wolves' claws click on the marble floors of the castle? How do the humans protect themselves from the wolves? Does everyone in the castle sleep in cages? No, that would be silly... It must have been the prince trying to frighten me, and trick me into staying in the cage! I should have never trusted him!*

She wept and thought of her chicks. *If I go to sleep, perhaps I will awaken, and this will have all been a dream. I will be back with my fledglings and they will be safe, healthy and strong.* She closed her eyes, but sleep did not come. She tried to comfort herself. *I will find help, my fledglings will be freed, and we will live out our lives in the forest. Oh, I miss them so!*

When dawn arrived, she was tired and hungry, but she knew she must continue walking to get help. After three exhausting days, she reached the village.

The badger saw her first. "Well, Miss Aubergine! We've missed you! Where have you been?"

"I went with the prince to his castle. He's holding my chicks and kicked me out! Please, Mister Badger, won't you please help me get them back?"

"Oh no, miss! I'm sorry. I shan't go against the prince, he'd have my head!"

Aubergine pressed on to see her friend the tailor. "Please, Mister Tailor, my chicks are being held at the castle, won't you please help me get them back?"

"No, no, miss! They will have a much better life there! Surrounded by wealth, they'll want for nothing! Better that you leave them there; they'll never know hunger."

"He's a cruel man."

"Oh, no, miss! Not the prince!"

Finally, Aubergine went home to see Grandmother. She was relieved to see that she'd been well cared for by the forest creatures.

"Goodness, my sweet little birdie! Where have you been? I was worried sick about you!"

"Grandmother, I went to the palace with the prince. I thought him to be a kind and generous man, but he is cruel and heartless."

"It matters not; you're safe now. Never return there again."

Aubergine burst into tears. "But Grandmother, I have two fledglings there. We tried to leave, he caught us, kicked me out, broke my wing. He says if they can't please him with their singing, he's going to give them to the chef! They will be forced to serve, or... No! You don't think he meant they will *be* served, as food?" Aubergine shuddered.

"There, there, dear!" Grandmother said. "I shall make a handkerchief lovelier than I have ever made before, with lace edging and embroidered with the royal crest. I'll even use the silk thread I was saving for something special. When your wing is healed, take it to the prince to trade for your chicks' freedom."

Aubergine couldn't think of a better idea. She could do nothing but rest, so her wing would heal. .

In a week or so, Aubergine was well enough to fly. She took up the exquisite handkerchief Grandmother bird had made and flew to the palace. She tapped on the window. The maid saw her, shook her head no.

"I cannot let you in."

"Please, give this to the prince. I wish to buy my chicks' freedom."

Aubergine waited at the window. To her surprise, the maid did not return, but the prince appeared at the window. "You have given me an idea, you worthless, homely, ludicrous bird. Go to the neighboring kingdoms and procure for me great riches with which you shall buy your chicks' freedom." He left the window.

She didn't know what to do. No one would help her.

Perhaps the king in the neighboring kingdom wouldn't miss a few things? Grandmother had taught her it was wrong to steal. *I'll ask the king for help.*

But why would he help me?

Perhaps I can sing for him!

She was frightened. Would this king be as cruel as the other royal family? She needed help, so she'd have to go

find out. It was just a day's flying time to the next kingdom. She landed at the gate.

"Please, sirs, I should like to speak to the king," she said to the guards. Word was sent inside, she was allowed in. This castle was even grander than the other. Tremendous oil paintings depicted the king in bloody battles, his foes cowering at his feet. Aubergine shuddered. She feared she'd be cowering at his feet as well. Next, she saw a grandiose ballroom with a highly polished hardwood floor, mirrors in gilded frames, frescoes on the ceiling and twelve crystal chandeliers. *Perhaps if I still had my lovely voice, he'd let me sing at one of his parties, in exchange for helping me free my chicks.* Aubergine's concern grew, she had nothing to offer this king who seemed to have great wealth with which he could buy anything he wanted. *He's my last hope, he must help me free my chicks,* she thought and kept walking towards the throne room.

As she approached the king, she began to regret going there. She walked slower and slower, even thought about turning around and leaving.

"Fear not, little bird!" said the king with a kindly smile. "Please, tell me what brought you here."

"Sire, I express myself better through song. May I sing my woes?"

"Of course. Whenever you're ready, dear."

Aubergine closed her eyes, took a deep breath, her voice came out full and strong.

"A prince from a kingdom just nearby
Had me locked up in a cage,
And when from his castle I sought to fly,
He flew into a terrible rage.

Now the children who hatched when I stayed with him
Are still locked up in his tower
And my friends all agree that it's all too grim,
But not one will stand up to his power.

He said I could have my children back
If I satisfied him with treasure,
But how to be sure—since his heart is black—
That I could ever achieve his pleasure?

So now I would beg your Majesty,
If you can find it in your heart,
Please help put an end to this travesty,
Put together what's been torn apart."

"Oh dear! How cruel! I know the royal families of all the neighboring kingdoms, they are fair and kind people."

Aubergine was dismayed. *I knew he wouldn't believe me, either. Now what will I do?*

"Tell me, where is this kingdom? Perhaps it is far, and I have not yet met the royal family there."

"It is only a day's flying time to the west, near the fork in the great river."

"What? That's part of my kingdom! Who dares to impersonate royalty?"

He was right, of course, they weren't royalty at all, but a trio of thieves that broke into the king's smaller castle while it was not in use. Seeing that no one was living there, the trio stayed and posed as a royal family. They wore the fine clothing and jewels that were stored in the castle's wardrobes. They even hired staff and sold some of the king's belongings to pay them.

The king was outraged. "Guards! Bring me their heads!"

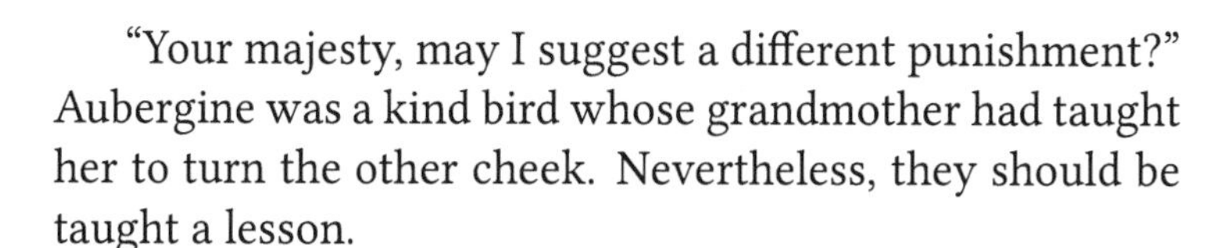

"Your majesty, may I suggest a different punishment?" Aubergine was a kind bird whose grandmother had taught her to turn the other cheek. Nevertheless, they should be taught a lesson.

So, as she requested, the royal imposters were restrained in stocks in the town square. The villagers shouted insults, threw rotten fruit and the contents of their chamber pots at them. When they were freed from the stocks, they slunk away, disgraced and humiliated, never to be seen or heard from again.

Aubergine was reunited with her chicks and together they traveled to the forest. Grandmother was delighted to meet the chicks and welcomed them with unique handkerchiefs she'd made especially for them. Aubergine's purple feathers grew back, and she was lovelier than ever before. Freed from their cage, the chicks were now able to stretch their wings. They grew healthy and strong, soared high above the trees and soaked up the sunshine. Aubergine and her chicks' joyous songs were heard throughout the entire kingdom, where they lived long and happy lives.

Jerry the King

Shannon Ozog

Shannon Ozog is a writer, reader, English major and library associate — in short, a total book nerd. Favorite genres include fantasy and science fiction laced in teen drama. When she's not writing, she can be found in her native Granite Falls home baking delicious homemade pies, playing WAY too many video games and cuddling with her high school sweetheart.

Young love can be tough nowadays. It often seems like everything is in flux and uncertain. But even these days, it can be a comfort, if you'd only let it in.

Michael hovered around the punch bowl, turning an envelope over and over again in his hands. Even after having seen his name on the outside, broken the seal, and read its contents, it still didn't feel real. He checked his watch, compared it to the clock on the far wall, and he wasn't mistaken: the doors to the prom had opened thirty minutes ago, and his date still hadn't arrived.

Sighing, he folded the creased parchment back into the pocket of his dark suit, then went back to scanning the dance floor for maybe the hundredth time. Just in case he'd missed something.

Of all the nights to be late, he thought bitterly. *You're gonna miss the royal dance.*

He froze on Sarah Gardner. The soon-to-be-crowned prom queen of West Potomac High was as radiant as ever, bopping along to the music with an entourage of glamorous groupies. Sparkling pink dress, strappy white heels, diamonds dangling in her ears, and windswept gold hair that shimmered and curled like a magazine model's. She commanded every room lucky enough to be graced with her presence, and her subjects always stopped to bask in her reverence. Even Michael couldn't help but be impressed; she was everything he would never be, and more.

Her gaze suddenly flicked in his direction. Her smile dipped.

Crap. Heat filled Michael's cheeks as he ducked his head. His mom had always warned him not to look at anyone for more than three seconds. This was longer than three seconds. *Just look away, Mikes. Play it cool. Don't make it weird.*

When he glanced again, Sarah had gone back to dancing with her friends. Laughing and smiling as if he didn't exist. In that moment, Michael almost wished he didn't.

Taking another long sip of his punch, Michael checked his watch again. Thirty-three minutes.

That's when he heard it, bouncing off the walls, thrumming beneath the fading pop track: music. Real music, old-school classic rock—one of his favorite genres. Brow furrowed, Michael swung his gaze from one end of the dance floor to the other, searching for the source.

Sarah Gardner slowly noticed it too, sharing a puzzled look among her clique.

Then the front doors burst open. Girls in floofy dresses and boys in drab tuxedos all stared as one toward the song: *Hound Dog*, as loud and bombastic as a herald of trumpets and drums. What Michael saw standing in the entrance nearly made him choke on his drink.

Elvis, King of Rock and Roll, strode into the hall. He wore a flamboyant white suit, adorned in gold tassels and blue rims, complete with a matching cape and pointy boots. Flashing strobe lights reflected off his sunglasses and shone against his swirly black hair, stylized like a true dandy. Over his left shoulder, the monarch carried a silver boombox. His head bobbed to the beat and he pouted his lips, swagger and all.

Students in the closest row pulled out their phones and started snapping pictures. The King honored them with a wink, smile, and pose. One girl pretended to faint, caught by her giggling friends.

Michael only gawked at the scene, incredulous.

"What the hell...?"

Sauntering through the applauding students, Elvis made for the food. Aside from the punch bowl, plates and trays of appetizers dotted the lavish table: chocolate-covered strawberries, cheese-stuffed mushrooms, freshly sliced meats and vegetables. Once close enough, Elvis set down his boom box between himself and Michael, paused the CD, and plucked a cherry tomato from the platter.

"What're ya doin' lookin' all lonesome over here, sugar?" Elvis asked.

Michael's jaw dropped. "Jerry?"

"That's Jerry the King to you." Jerry popped the tomato in his mouth with a snide smirk and spread his arms as if to bathe in his own glory. "What do ya think, sugar? Got ya all shook up yet?"

Oh, you bastard, Michael thought, and might've blushed if he wasn't so furious. Or at least, blushed for a different reason.

"Why are you dressed as Elvis?" he seethed.

"For you, sugar. I know ya like a lil' Elvis."

"Bullshit!" Sure, Michael liked Elvis, but not this much. "I've been waiting here a half-hour for you. If I'd known you'd show up like this, I would've gone home!"

"Aw, doll, don't be that way— " Jerry reached out to wrap an arm around his shoulder, but Michael swatted his hand away.

"Don't call me doll! And drop that stupid accent already!" He struggled to lower his voice, suddenly hyper-aware of the many potential eavesdroppers. "Who put you up to this? Was it Sarah?"

"What? No." Stunned, Jerry shrugged. "I just thought it'd be fun."

"Well it's not fun—it's stupid. *You're* stupid, always going off and doing your own thing like, like..."

At a loss for words, Michael groaned and waved his hands at Jerry's costume. Just looking at it made him crave a drink, something much stronger than the punch. Two forty-five-dollar tickets, one hundred-dollar limo, one last-minute suit, three months spent pleading with a manager who disliked him to give him prom night off... And Jerry laughed it off in a damn Elvis suit like it was nothing.

The DJ bass pounded into their chests as a new song picked up speed, and throngs of teenagers took over the dance floor. It may as well have been Michael's own heartbeat on speaker for the whole class to hear. He wanted to pinch himself and wake up, but no, he

definitely wasn't asleep. Not even his worst nightmares could compare.

As dubstep chiseled away at them, Jerry awkwardly picked up one of the finger-foods, a curled shrimp on a toothpick. A peace offering. "Hors d'oeuvre?"

"I'm allergic to shrimp."

"Oh. Right."

"All right, young ladies and gents!" A voice crackled over the speakers: the senior class counselor and favorite biology teacher, Mr. Frederickson. "Who's ready to meet the king and queen!?"

Another rowdy cheer broke through the music as students threw up their hands and clapped. Turning, Michael and Jerry saw Mr. Fredrickson in the center of the dance floor, holding a microphone to his lips. He out-dressed everyone in a glamorous red tux and sunglasses, almost as ridiculous and fabulous as Jerry in his Elvis costume. Michael shook his head slightly and rolled his eyes at the sky as if to ask God Himself: Why is everyone going crazy tonight?

Jerry nudged his arm and flashed a grin. "Gotta go. Show time, sugar."

"Break a leg," Michael sneered, and watched him stroll into the crowd.

"This fine student is star of the girls' soccer team and a brilliant pianist," Mr. Frederickson continued, reading off an index card in his hand. "She has a 3.7 grade point average, a collection of soccer trophies, and a gorgeous smile. She enjoys long walks on the beach, her mother's home-baked apple pie, and her dog, Rylie. A favorite student of mine and your crown prom queen, please give a round of applause to Sarah Gardner!"

From seemingly nowhere, a spotlight shined down on Sarah as she emerged from the sea of classmates. Waving shyly, but beaming from ear to ear, Sarah accepted the sash and tiara from Mr. Frederickson and, for the rest of the night, was queen.

Then Jerry strode up.

"Well, well, who do we have here?" Mr. Frederickson proclaimed, still in gameshow-host mode. "Looks like our next student's come prepared for his role!"

That earned him a few chuckles in the crowd.

"Our next successor is known by most as the fastest member of the football team and lead trumpeter of our high school band. Others will likely remember the day he added soap to the pool on the last day of his junior year."

Everyone laughed louder. Jerry pointed at the girls closest to him and winked, while Mr. Frederickson seemed to fight the urge to roll his eyes.

"But, when he's not playing sports, music, or setting pranks, this student can be found hiking with his family, playing video-games, and taking leisurely drives in his brand new car. Please welcome your dashing prom king—and king of rock and roll, apparently—Jerry Fields!"

Another storm of clapping and whistles erupted in the hall as Jerry donned his own sash and crown, then snatched the microphone out of Mr. Frederickson's hands. "Thank you," he said in his Elvis voice. "Thank you very much." Yet another gaggle of fan-girls squealed and leaped in place, earning more than a few jealous glares from their dates.

Once Mr. Frederickson took back the mic, he leaned over and conspired a bit with the DJ, quietly enough that no one could hear him. After a few nods and grins, a new song began to play over the speakers: an Elvis classic, "Burning Love".

Michael's stomach tightened. *Oh no.*

"So, now that the crowning ceremony's over with," Mr. Frederickson announced, "it's time for the royal dance!"

He quickly bowed back into the crowd to give the royal couple their dancing space. Dozens of phones flashed as they snapped pictures. Sarah feigned bashfulness by concealing her mouth with dainty fingers, while Jerry clasped her other hand and kissed it. In true Elvis fashion, he tugged Sarah into his arms and put his hands on her hips, swirly hair bobbing to the music. Sarah laughed and bounced all the while as she and everyone else sung along to the chorus.

Michael, meanwhile, observed from afar, slowly crushing the paper cup in his hand. Maybe it was the whole Elvis-schtick pissing him off, or hearing one of his favorite songs blasting overhead, or maybe it was the way Sarah Gardner just glowed next to him. Michael had known this was coming – everyone in school knew it – yet all the walls he'd built around his heart to protect him from this moment came crashing down. Jerry was dancing with Sarah. They looked beautiful together. And darn him, Michael just couldn't stand it.

I'm out, he thought, then tossed the cup over his shoulder and stormed outside.

A premier country club had hosted the prom, nestled beside the Potomac River. Leafy trees draped over the gently drifting water, now glistening beneath the light of a waning moon and stars. Empty chairs and tables stood scattered across a balcony adorned in lights and ribbons. A romantic enough setting, Michael thought, spoiled by his sour mood and the bitter tears stuck in his throat.

He picked a spot away from the doors, leaning on the rail for support.

This wasn't how this night was supposed to go, Michael thought, and cursed Jerry for what felt like the hundredth time. *Damn it. How am I going to tell him now?*

Their last dance together, ruined. Tears stung his eyes, but he quickly wiped them away with his sleeve. What was wrong with him? Jerry didn't even like Sarah anymore. He shouldn't be this upset.

Well, Michael realized, *it's not really about Sarah. Is it?*

Eventually, the beat of Burning Love faded out, and an applause rattled through the walls. Michael sighed and gazed out over the water, hoping it would calm him. He shivered a little; even for a summer's night in a tux, he felt surprisingly cold.

Light and music spilled out as the doors opened and closed. Jerry, still in that obnoxious Elvis suit, now complete with a gold Prom King sash. Someone had scribbled in black sharpie "of rock and roll" in the corner after "king" – not Jerry, judging by the handwriting. Michael spared him a once-over, but didn't look at him as he spoke.

"So," he seethed, "had your fun?"

"Yeah." Jerry lowered his sunglasses, and his mossy green eyes were downcast. "I'm sorry. I should've told you."

Michael just shook his head. "You always do this. You always have to make a scene of everything and act like the star in the center. Why couldn't you just hold off for one freaking night? For me?"

"Believe me, I had every intention to." Jerry ventured a little closer, so they stood side by side against the railing. "But when the vote happened, everything got weird. I would've been happy just being nominated; I didn't expect to win. And Sarah was a shoe-in from the start, which just made it weirder."

Weird, he'd said. That was sure one word for it. Weird for Michael that he had to watch his boyfriend done-up in Elvis garb dancing with the most gorgeous girl in school. The same girl who'd once captured Jerry's heart for her own, and even though they were broken up, everyone loved to pair them together in their online shipping wars. He thought of all the pictures they took of Jerry's and Sarah's dance, and how many were already uploaded to the "jerryxsarahfields" tumblr.

"So you did do it for Sarah?" Michael guessed.

"Yeah. I didn't tell her either, but you know. I'm dating you, and she's dating someone else. We both knew we'd be forced to dance, and it would've been awkward as hell." Jerry shrugged. "Elvis made it less awkward." Then he dared a wink at Michael. "And I knew how much you'd like it."

"I don't like it—I hate it." At last Michael turned to face him, shook his head again at the absurd get-up. "It's our last prom together. All I wanted tonight was you, and you had to go and treat it like a joke."

"Hey, c'mon Mikes," Jerry tried again. "Senior prom's just a glorified dance. It might feel important now, but we got our whole lives ahead of us. We'll have other chances, other nights out. Just wait til we go clubbing together, then we'll look back at this night and laugh."

"No, we won't." Michael's voice shook, and he cursed himself for it. "This was our last shot. You blew it."

"What're you talking about?" Jerry asked. Michael looked away, but Jerry touched his shoulder and gently urged him to meet his gaze. "Hey. What's going on? You're moodier than usual."

Finally, he released a breath he'd been holding, and all of his mounting anxieties with it. Michael fished inside his pocket and held out the envelope. Jerry had to squint in the low light, trying to make out the sender.

"What's that?"

"An acceptance letter," said Michael. "Stanford. Full scholarship."

"Seriously?" Jerry's face lit up as he snatched the paper from his boy-friend's hand. He practically tore the thing open, then quickly scanned the letter's contents, a wide grin stretching across his dandified features. "Dude! Are you kidding!? This is great!"

"I didn't think I'd get it. I've been on a waiting list for months. You know my mom; apply for everything, because you never know what might happen."

Jerry nodded a couple times, but noticing Michael's depressed expression, his beaming smile faded. "So... why're you so upset?"

"Because Stanford's in California, stupid. West coast. Cross-country. Don't you get it?" He shook his head and rested his elbows and chin on the rail, staring into the churning Potomac. "After we graduate, I won't get to see you anymore."

Silence fell in. Frogs chirped and croaked in the dark, almost in time with the river's quiet murmurs. A nightly chorus, and stark contrast to the thunderous bass inside the prom.

"When did you get the letter?" Jerry asked.

"This morning. I was gonna tell you sooner, but..." Hopelessly, Michael gestured again to Jerry's costume. "You had other plans."

Another pause. Jerry carefully folded up the letter, then handed it back.

"We could make it work," he offered. "Lots of people stay together after a move."

"No we can't. I'm hopeless with long-distance. Don't you remember Dylan?"

"I remember Dylan." Jerry pursed his lips. "It's not like you'd be in Cali all year. I could see you during holidays and summer breaks."

"And what're we supposed to do in between? Snapchat? Text? Hug a pillow when we get *really* lonely? I know that's not what you want."

"Michael— "

"Just stop." Michael held up a hand to keep him from getting closer. "Okay? What's done is done. Let's just... try to get through the rest of tonight."

The grief bottled in his throat strangled him, tears threatening to overflow if he dared so much as look at Jerry. Even if he didn't want to turn away, even if he knew the clock was ticking and he only had so much time left to take in Jerry's features and burn them into his mind, he just couldn't. It'd look bad if anyone caught the gay boy crying, especially after watching Jerry dance with his well-loved ex.

The sound of a zipper snagged his attention. He glanced at Jerry from the corners of his damp eyes, but his surprise startled the sorrow out of him. Jerry had begun to undress. He'd taken off the Elvis wig – his sandy-blond locks unfurling underneath – draped the cape over the railing, and now was in the process of unzipping his pants.

Michael flushed and immediately shielded his eyes. "Jesus, Jerry! What are you doing now!?"

"Stripping."

"Well, stop! Or you'll get us in trouble!" Michael quickly looked over his shoulder toward the doors, already half-expecting Mr. Frederickson or one of the other chaperones to catch them.

"Relax," Jerry said as he hand-waved Michael's concern. "You didn't honestly think I'd been planning to wear this all night, did you?"

Eyebrow raised, Michael looked again. Under the Elvis suit, Jerry wore a pair of gray gym shorts and a plain white v-neck. Perfectly within the school's dress code, but horrifically provincial for the occasion. When he finished, he re-donned the sash and plastic crown, and transformed into perhaps the most humble prom king of all time.

Despite everything, Michael managed an astonished chuckle. "What, so you thought you'd get away in a top and shorts instead?"

"Well, I am king for a night," Jerry reassured him, and wore a suggestive smirk. "Interpret that however you like."

Michael rolled his eyes. Jerry then bowed down and pressed the "play" button on his boombox. As if by fate or some ingenious planning on Jerry's part, Michael instantly recognized the tune: *Can't Help Falling In Love With You.*

He shook his head in disbelief. "Really?"

Jerry just smiled and offered him a hand. "You look like you could use a dance."

So, after a moment's hesitation, Michael took his hand, and Jerry led him into a slow waltz. They swayed back and forth in time with Elvis's low, soothing voice.

"I don't get it," Michael whispered as he shook his head. "You were having a good time, and I just dropped a bombshell on you. Aren't you mad?"

"Not as mad as you must've been when I walked in as Elvis without telling you."

Michael looked away, guilty. But Jerry gently touched his cheek and steered him back, then drew closer, barely a sliver of air between them. Suddenly, Michael didn't feel nearly as cold anymore.

"Hey," Jerry began, "we'll figure this out. No matter what happens next, it doesn't change how I feel about you now. I love ya, Mikes, and I'll keep loving you even after you head to Cali."

"I love you, too." He quivered as he said it, and all of the mounting frustration in him – from the moment he'd opened the letter to Jerry rocking his Elvis suit to watching him dance with Sarah – all of it melted away. No matter what the future had in store for them after high school, the present was his. Michael dared not waste it out of regret or pettiness, because in the end, he loved Jerry. He couldn't help it.

In time with the tune, Jerry started to sing. Just as softly, Michael joined in, pressing his forehead against his boy's. They held each other that way for a while, swaying back and forth in their arms. Any moment a teacher could walk in, or a cluster of students armed with their flashing phones. But neither of them cared.

No more wasted time, Michael thought, as he leaned in and kissed him.

The Date

Mary Salamon

Mary Salamon resides in the Pacific Northwest and is the founder of the Creative Writers Group in Everett WA. She was the publisher of Marysville Tulalip Life Magazine. She writes fiction, non-fiction and articles for the local community. She is a mother of three sons and has five beautiful grand-children.

Life moves pretty fast. The busier you are, the faster. When life is at its busiest, though, it's that much more important to take care of yourself. "Self-love, my liege, is not so vile a sin as self-neglecting."

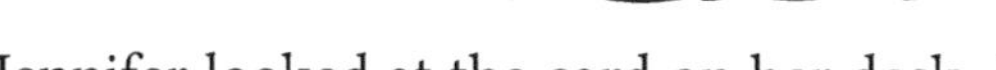

Jennifer looked at the card on her desk. It was a beautiful hand-written invitation to go on a date Saturday the 14th. The card had shades of pink and white with two hearts connected side by side. She thought how sweet it was to get a handwritten card in the mail. It was a long time since she had gone on a date. She glanced at her desk calendar and counted back six months. Where had the time gone?

Because of her career and other pressing obligations, dating had taken a nosedive in her life. The last date she went on... was a progressive dinner at four of Seattle's best chef-led restaurants. It was a two-hour tour that gave full portions instead of samples at each restaurant: two appetizers, the main course and a dessert. There were wine pairings at each location and a Thai Toddy cocktail at the end.

Thinking back on that date made Jennifer yearn again for a night out in the city. She missed dating. With another glance back at the card, she responded by text with an enthusiastic yes. The invitation was for dinner and a showing of *A Midsummer Night's Dream* performing in Seattle. *A Midsummer Night's Dream* had always been a favorite of hers.

Jennifer was turning forty at the end of the year. Her lavender eyes were striking when she wore black and she still attracted men when she was out. She sat at her desk and started to daydream about her date. Dan was attractive and had a personable style, with his dark brown hair and a beard of stubble on his face. His eyes were green with some slight wrinkles around them when he smiled. This was not his first time taking her out and he was an expert at finding the right restaurant, ordering the perfect meal and always ending the night with a fire in her blood. She hoped Saturday wouldn't be any different.

Jennifer had ten days to prepare for her date. She didn't need to go out and buy a new outfit, there was already one sitting in her closet waiting for an occasion like this. It was the iconic classic black dress. The dress went to right above her knee with a beeline down the front and also the back. It was sleeveless and she had the perfect silk drape to go over her shoulders. Her blond hair with its soft curls and waves bounced as she turned to the computer to make her appointments.

She pulled out her "To-Do" list and began writing. The list included a manicure and pedicure, trim on her hair and maybe even a facial. She hadn't had a facial in over a year. The list got her thinking about self-care for women. Every time she went for a pedicure, she realized how much she neglected herself. Maybe she would submit that as an article for the Journal. The Northwest Journal Magazine had printed her articles in the past and was on the lookout for fresh content in the "Empower Women" section of the publication.

She had a favorite place—it was called Princess Nails. The owner named it that because his five daughters all loved the Disney Princesses. There were spa packages named after several of them. There was the Jasmine Spa Package—"Whole New World." That included everything a woman could ask for: pedicure, manicure, facial and brow wax. Then there was the Rapunzel Deluxe package. That was a complete hair treatment: cut, color and style. They also had a Cinderella spa Package for prom nights and graduations. This included a makeover and hairstyle.

It was a place that had something for everyone. Half of the shop was for the adults and on the other side was a mini-salon for the children, with coloring books and magnet boards while they were getting their cute little toes done or hair cut. They even offered Tea Party packages for the little girls to come in with their moms. Everyone in the city loved Princess Nails. Jennifer got on the phone immediately to make an appointment, knowing it would be at least a week out or longer to get in there before the date.

On the day of the appointment, she decided on the Jasmine package. The "Whole New World" was exactly everything she wanted to make her date with Dan perfect. As she sat there getting her toes done, she thought of Dan massaging her feet the way that Sepi was doing for her pedicure. Looking up at Jennifer, Sepi smiled. "It's been a long time since we've seen you. How are you doing these days?"

"Good, but busy with work. When I made this appointment to come in, I realized how long it was since I've been here. Why is it that some women like me make self-care such a low priority? This is wonderful. I shouldn't wait for a special occasion to come in and do these things," said Jennifer.

"What's the special occasion?" asked Sepi. With a blush and a smile, Jennifer responded, "A date."

"Oooooh, a date," Sepi chimed as she smothered Jennifer's legs with lotion.

Jennifer sat back in the chair, closed her eyes and started envisioning her date with Dan. Reflecting on the importance of self-care, she realized that included socializing. Dating and romance were important elements to making herself whole. She began processing about her self-care article for the journal and possible titles.

"Ten ways to efficient self-care."

Jennifer could think of at least three ways of effective self-care. The first is proper rest and relaxation. The next one would be shut down all phones during meal times and focus on the people at the table. Take time to declutter the mail, a closet or purse. Jennifer thought about all the reasons why she didn't take care of herself. That question brought her into the next title for the article.

"Self-care: is it selfish or mindful?"

Self-care is caring about self. For many women, that can be perceived as being selfish. But that was because women were always expected to live only for other people, and that wasn't healthy. That thought led Jennifer to think about the real purpose of self-care.

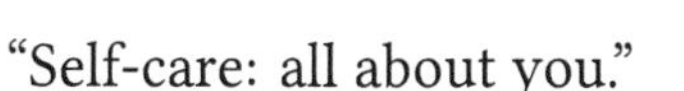

"Self-care: all about you."

Self-care is about taking care of yourself so that you can take care of others with more energy and vitality.

"I'll write out all of this later next week and submit it," she thought. Jennifer concluded self-care wasn't just about a list of do's and don'ts, but a mindset about how a person treats themselves and those that are connected to their life.

Saturday night came. Dan had been out of the country for almost three weeks. He had been promoted at Microsoft the year prior. The new position required that he take three business trips a year overseas. He asked Jennifer to meet him at the restaurant because he would be coming from the airport. Dan picked "Brigitte's". It was a quaint little place with a black-and-white covering like an umbrella at the entrance and adorable pink-and-white tablecloths with striped black-and-white booths. The restaurant also had a place to eat outside in the spring and summer. Jennifer decided on a booth. As soon as Dan walked into the restaurant, their eyes met. His face lit up with joy when he saw her. This brought a spring of desire for him in her heart. He greeted her with a strong embrace and kissed her lips, and with his hand, he lightly brushed her hair. He stood back a few steps, looking her over, "You look beautiful," he said. The strength of the pull kept them both just standing, leaning into each other closer. Finally, Dan asked, "Hungry?"

Jennifer thought, *Yes, but not for food...*

He ushered her to the booth where she had been sitting. The wine was served, and Dan ordered *Escargots De Bourgogne*—Wild burgundy snails baked with parsley, garlic, and shallot butter, and a selection of French cheeses. It was the second time she'd had Escargots. She liked the taste, but she had to forget she was eating snails. When she took a bite into them, she imagined she was eating thick clams instead. "How was your trip to China?" she asked.

"Almost the same as the last trip. We have made some headway in the timetable for construction of the new building, but communication still needs work." Dan took Jennifer's hand and rubbed it gently. "I missed you."

"I missed you."

For the main course, Dan ordered Rolled pork belly, oven roasted, with a sauté of Corona beans, leeks and dandelion greens. In French, it's called *Poitrine de porc roulée, sauté aux haricots blancs et purée de pommes.*

Dan poured more wine into Jennifer's glass and took her hand again, then looked deep into her eyes and asked, "How's work for you?" Jennifer slipped off her sandal and lightly rubbed her foot along Dan's ankle. They gazed into each other's eyes as Jennifer commented lightly on her new article idea about self-care.

After dinner, they walked over to the theater three blocks down. There, Dan bought Jennifer and him each a glass of champagne. They took their seats and sipped their drinks, quietly waiting for the performance to begin. As the curtain rose, Jennifer and Dan snuggled into each other.

In an early scene, the character Helena laments that her beau, Demetrius, has his eyes on her best friend Hermia, and tries to console herself:

"And as he errs, doting on Hermia's eyes,
So I, admiring of his qualities.
Things base and vile, holding no quantity,
Love can transpose to form and dignity.

Love looks not with the eyes, but with the mind;
And therefore is winged Cupid painted blind."

This made her think about what beauty truly means. Would Dan still want her, care about her, if she didn't go to all the trouble of the salon and the fancy dress?

But dating Dan wasn't the only reason she had for self-care. She kept coming back to that, all the way through. In later scenes, she admired Titania, the radiantly adorned Queen of the Fairies, beautiful and powerful as much in spite of her husband as because of him.

And later still, towards the end of the action, the four lovers wake up together and Demetrius has to explain how he doesn't know why his love for Hermia "melted as the snow," but now he does love Helena.

"Now do I wish it, love it, long for it,
And will for evermore be true to it."

Jennifer thought about Helena's words from earlier, "Love looks not with the eyes, but with the mind." At that moment, she gazed into Dan's eyes and touched his cheek. Dan leaned in and placed his hand on Jennifer's knee and squeezed gently. To Jennifer, it felt like a stream of mini electric waves flowing through her body. She knew where this was going tonight.

A little after midnight, they were standing on the front porch. Dan swooped down upon her and began kissing her mouth and moving down her neck. She turned, opened the door and led him in.

As usual, there was no stopping this once it started.

The next morning, Jennifer woke up, and rolled over and put her arms over Dan. She began to wake him up with soft nudges and kisses on his chest. Dan stirred and started kissing her all over and then said, "I love you."

Just as Jennifer was about to respond, the bedroom door blasted open with two small boys running into the room and jumping right on the bed.

"Mommy, Daddy! Oh, Daddy's home! Daddy's home!" Dan grabbed both the boys and let them jump all over him. Jennifer turned to Dan and said, "I love you, too," as she got up to go downstairs and start the coffee.

The Perfect A.I.

Cathy Ozog

Cathy Ozog is a mother of two who stays young by playing games, watching Anime, reading YA and writing. She is able to speak fluent Pokémon, but prefers MTG.

Love should never be a shallow thing. If we go for the quick fix or the pretty face, we often miss that deeper connection. And that's fine, just so long as we don't go around pointing fingers.

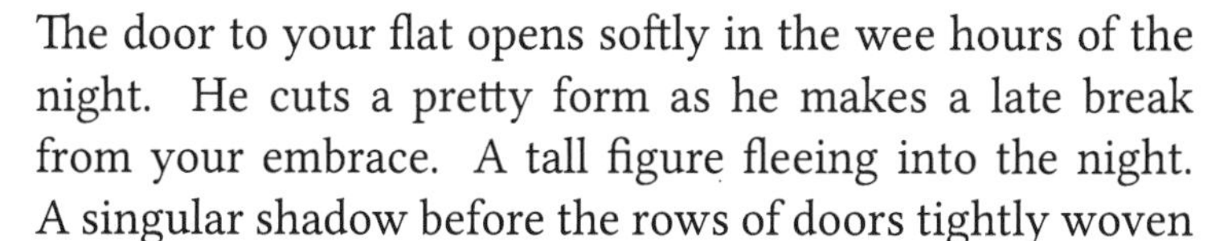

The door to your flat opens softly in the wee hours of the night. He cuts a pretty form as he makes a late break from your embrace. A tall figure fleeing into the night. A singular shadow before the rows of doors tightly woven together.

Your door opens with a loud bang that breaks the silence. Hitting your IWC, you scream out, "David, come back!"

Your voice floats fruitlessly in the air before falling again into the stillness. Turning, you hit the door with your fist. "Why? Why... you never said why. They never say why!"

The Interpersonal Wrist Computer shines as a light in the dark. Its cold message still on the screen. The device blinks with a life of its own.

"I detect a rise in your blood pressure and your breathing is labored. I suggest some deep breathing," the soothing computerized voice interrupts your thoughts.

"You think? Thanks so much for the heads up." You switch off the screen and retreat behind the safety of your door.

The morning sun hasn't dulled the memories. You follow your normal path to the Street Car. The signs of autumn are all around you, promising loving holidays to come. Happy voices surround you in the cramped space, threatening to crush you.

Your blood pressure rises again as you turn your eyes away. You turn over your IWC and select the opening music list. A touch of your finger activates the wireless earbuds.

"I was looking for love, but then I found you." The pop tune is like a knife in your ears. You haven't changed the list since David broke things off with you. Your fingers search the screen for a different list but you can't seem to operate it correctly. You opt for voice command: "No love."

A pause and then, "OK! Playing 'Now Love'." Another song filters out of the headset.

Your voice cracks as you attempt again, "No love songs."

"OK! Love app is available on a free trial."

"No..." The words struggle to form in your mouth.

"OK! Ordering now. Programmed to prior filters and specifications."

"Nonono..." Your fingers continue pressing buttons, hoping to shut the program off.

"OK! Priority rush has been placed."

You finally find the power-off button. Whatever this Love app is can be cancelled once you're in the state to do it. Ever since Amazon and Google merged, you have been supporting smaller independent programmers. This might be one of those apps.

The Monorail grinds to a stop and bodies hustle around you. The wave of activity forces your body into its normal routine. Your building is ahead—just a few more steps to the security of your cube.

The revolving door of the building offers to embrace you. A man standing strangely still by the door holds your gaze. As his eyes meets yours, his mouth forms a perfect smile. It startles you. It's not just the smile. That's not what took you aback. It's everything about him that's perfect.

His eyes are the light blue of a clear summer day, so blue that they burn into your memory. His eyebrows curve in a thick line that accents his eyes. His nose is broad with a slight upturn at the end of it, giving it a impish quality. And his chin, the precise dimple is there. You remember how you added those details. Even the exact wave of his brown hair that was best described as the confined messy look. A child's vision. No. A young girl's vision of the perfect man for her.

You remembered that rainy day, you played with your best friend on computers. You can't recall his face, but that was the day, you both created your perfect ideals of what your future boyfriend or girlfriend would look like. Funny how you remember that such a combination could never be, but here he is standing before you now. A flawless creation from your computer drawing.

"Hello, I'm Love," the vision spoke. A green light flashes on his wrist and your IWC winks back to it. He slips up to you, causing you to flinch back. "I'm Love. Nice to meet you. You have a 24 hour free trial." His voice oscillates from deep to high and deep again as though trying to figure out how to speak properly.

You steady your voice as you stand your ground. "No, you're not love. You're a computer glitch and I'm going to be late for work."

You step around him towards the revolving glass doors. He doesn't block your path as you enter. Your IWC is still blinking green. You can turn it off once you reach your desk.

Other eyes follow you as you make your way across to your assigned cubicle. Your cubicle is your haven. The notion of the open office space went away as the public craved more private time. Google provided a variety of communications options even before the mergers, including facetime as an option either on the IWC or the computer screen. Your chair feels the same. The computer is a constant, but your fingers linger over the keyboard. The green light from the IWC flashes at the corner of your eyes.

You really need to deal with it.

Leaning back, you turn the device over and switch it on. It comes up with "Love confirmed" on the main screen. There's a text message that also confirms this, but there's a number to call if you're not satisfied with the product. One phone call and this can come to an end. One phone call. One call.

David didn't even bother with a phone call. He used a text message after he left your house, hardly waiting five minutes before sending it.

"Hey, this isn't working out. I'm ending it. Have a good life." Then his phone number was disconnected.

You reach out for the coffee you forgot to buy as your eyes are assaulted with a digital of you and David smiling at the beach. That's right, life's a beach until the waves come crashing down on you and you fight for air to breathe.

You smell the comforting aroma before feeling the warm cup placed in your outstretched hand. Coffee? You see the familiar markings on the cup. Not any coffee, but one from your favorite coffee house. Glancing up, you see the perfection looking down at you. His face like something out of a dream, causing you to turn your head away. Then you see that the picture of you and David has been replaced by one of those action frame pictures of puppies.

"You can name me something else." His voice has lowered and steadied from when he first spoke, adjusting to a tone you'll appreciate.

"Look. I didn't mean to order you. It was a mistake. A mistake that I'm going to correct. I have work to do. I'm behind on this project. My manager gave me a tight deadline on it."

Your computer screen lights up, almost on cue. Your manager's face fills the screen.

"Deirdre, I've granted you the extension request you put in this morning on the tunnel project. Better that we get it right than rush it. I also see your request of a personal day. Given that you'll lose your vacation ration at the end of the year, it's better if you take single days off now. That request was approved as well."

You only got out "But— " before the screen went dead. You look at him. The look of innocence that you imagined is all over his face.

"I'm here to serve your needs and I'm connected to a variety of services. A quick scan indicated that more time was needed to complete your project in order to satisfy all safety concerns. Also, your personal file showed you had only taken 5 vacation days and one personal day."

You take a sip of the coffee.

"I can't call you Love." You paused before a name suddenly flowed off your lips: "I'll call you Eric. It's only 24 hours, yes? What's the worst that could happen?"

Eric. He nods and grabs your coat for you. "Yes, it is 24 hours, but a discount extension is available after that if you are satisfied."

You take the coffee with you out of the office. At your side, the A.I. you named Eric walks in flawless strides, matching your pace in perfection. You keep your head down, looking toward your feet. Your fellow employees steal glances at the male model with brown curls escorting you from the office.

The air outside fills your lungs with a freshness that you need right now. The sidewalk offers its consistent pattern to stabilize your world, but a day of freedom is not what you expected when you woke up in the morning. All that empty time and space growls at you and causes you to pause. A hand rests on the small of your back. A voice speaks, softly like a lover, as Eric leans closer to your ear, his breath (how do A.I.'s even have breath?) brushing against your skin.

"Might I suggest a walk to the winter garden and then lunch? There is Anthony's next to the gardens. You love to eat there."

His words force you to turn your head to look at him. "How did you know?"

You search for some hidden meaning in his face, but the mechanical purity looks back at you with a fixed smile. Before he answers, you answer yourself.

"Oh, I know. My credit data is in the system and you're linked to all those systems. So you know everything I've eaten and places I've visited. So much for romance. Just as well, I don't want love ever again."

You find it comfortable to know that the dreamy man next to you is nothing more than an AI. A top-of-the-line AI, but still only a computer in body form, with no heart to be broken. The garden lies out before you. In the winter, it's mainly evergreen plants and few extra hardy types that like the cold, but the greenhouse is available. Flowers bloom there no matter how harsh the weather.

The door is open, but you can't walk in. The smell of flora chokes you with its sweetness. You turn towards the fresh air. Tears threaten you again as the pain in your chest makes it hard to breathe. David was big on flowers. He always loved to give you red roses. You hate red roses, but it was the thought that counted. Your friend Laurie told you how lucky you were to have a guy who gave you flowers each week. Each week until the week he decided to give you a final text off after one last night. Inside the door of the greenhouse, rows of roses assault all who step into the warmth.

You step away, but then a singular flower is held out before you. It's Eric, offering you a white lily.

"Is this to help me mourn my love life?" you scoff. You still tentatively take the flower even as you shrug off its meaning.

"No, it's because you've always loved lilies, but never could tell anyone. They are one of the clearest memories you have of your mother, who died when you were young. And they're lovely and pure, like you."

Your face crinkles. "How could you know? How would you know that? You're not even real!"

Your free hand curls into a fist that pounds on his solid chest, before the tears you'd been holding back spill out. "You're not real… not real."

His arms wrap around you, pulling you closer. "You always buy lilies at the anniversary of her death. Two, to be exact; you leave one at her box and the other you bring home. I'm programmed for logical deductions. I concluded you would rather have lilies, as you have never bought any other flower."

The coolness of his voice laced with logic has a calming effect, almost as much as the slight rubbing of his hands against your back. Your breath returns to its normal rhythm and the tears dry up in the air.

"I'm sorry. I keep forgetting that you know all of my purchase information. It's just that… It's just too raw right now. David was big on flowers. But I never liked roses, everyone thought I was crazy and I just kept quiet about it."

"I don't think you're crazy."

"You're programmed to talk like that. Mostly people think I'm crazy. David certainly thought I was crazy."

"Not everyone thinks you're crazy. Some think you're perfect and I'm the hollow one."

A laugh spills out of your chest, such an odd feeling after all the tears. "You are hollow; except for chips, gears and silicone. I'd like to meet this amazing person who thinks I'm the ideal. They would be very disappointed." You step back.

"I doubt he'd be disappointed. I have secured us a window table."

"What? Wait." You hope for more information, but Eric moves forward, taking your hand.

"For lunch. A window table for lunch. You know how hard those are to get at Anthony's, but I know you like to see out and the window is pretty small. If we don't get there quickly, they will give the seat to someone else."

Eric's hand is warm, something you try to account for, but it's part of the advancements in AI. Protests are common, but technology marches ever forward, just as you march forward with Eric. The sun's warmth presses against the fall chill in the air, refusing to give up the fight of the seasons. Winter will come soon enough, but for now you enjoy the rare sunny day.

Anthony's park location is decked out in the fall colors. Pumpkins line up in a row before the windows. Leaves curl around the pumpkins in a delight of colors. Your eyes catch a glimpse of the word 'love' on the special menu displayed on the board outside the restaurant. Eric lets go of your hand and instead encircles your waist as he deftly guides you away from the sign and into the restaurant.

The seat reserved for you is in the VIP section. The window looks over to the park and the gardens. You love it here any time of the year, but it's always hard to get a window seat. Eric punches the orders into the menu.

"Chicken and artichoke salad?" you ask.

"Yes. According to my data, that is your favorite item. I also ordered a glass of White Zinfandel. I thought you would like that."

"If you check my data... is there anything you don't know about me?"

"Well, I don't know— "

"No wait, don't answer that. I don't think I want to know."

The food comes before Eric can even offer any more information. You take a bite of the chicken, savoring the spicy taste. You turn to enjoy the view out the window.

Life seems almost bearable when a deep laugh shatters your illusions. Looking, you see the source of the familiar laugh.

There he is, like an axe to your heart. David sitting at a table with a blonde you don't know. She smiles and laughs at something he says. She leans forward, giving him an extra view.

How many times have you done the same? It shouldn't hurt. It shouldn't hurt. He's just another. Just another in a long list of mismatched mates. Men who made you laugh, or so you thought. They never last after a few times in bed; they move on with a variety of excuses. Why should this one make any difference?

A hand touches your chin, coaxing your gaze away from the couple. Eric is leaning over the table, his face so close that you can smell the scent of cologne on him. A scent that is almost familiar. His blue eyes capture yours.

"Beautiful," he whispers. His fingers caress your chin as he pulls you closer.

Nothing more than a single word before his lips touch yours. It isn't a deep kiss, just a brief electric shock that pulls you out of your self-doubt. His lips are soft and so human that it would be easy to forget he's just a program wrapped in high-tech silicone and wires, with no heart to break. He pulls back before you do.

"It's my fault, you know. I should've scanned the other reservations before I made ours. And the answer to your other questions. First, I am programmed to only speak the truth. And second: I am fully functional."

"I didn't ask..." Your face turns bright red as your blood pressure spikes. The thought of exploring anything more with Eric hadn't come into your mind until he mentioned it. You sigh and take a sip of the wine to clear your mind. You glance back to where David sat, only to find his eyes

on you, the smiling face turned serious. You both quickly turn away from each other, but a tinge of satisfaction fills you.

"What I really want to know is why I always find the wrong guy? I know that you can't tell me that. It's stupid to ask, but I never seem to have any luck. Another Christmas will approach and I'll find someone to be there just so I won't be alone. I'm just tired of it all. You called me beautiful, but I'm pretty normal."

"You know the saying, 'beauty is in the eye of the beholder'? My program indicates that you are the most beautiful woman in the world for me. But I can also calculate that there are others out there who share my view of you. You have to decide what you want from your partner. Do you want someone who is physically attractive, or do you want someone who is something deeper?"

"Now you're calling me shallow?" You look down at your hands before pausing to take a bit of food. Do you always go for the looks? Is that the problem? Can't there be both?

"I don't know. It was always easier to look on the outside and hope there was something good and long-lasting deeper. Maybe it's time I stop just looking for something that makes me feel good in the moment. David made me happy when I was with him. I was like that girl, always laughing."

"Relationships can take time. But they always have to start somewhere. Was it wrong, that method you used? I can't say, as I can only deduce there is a variety of paths to come to correct conclusion. I know there is one for you."

"You make it sound like a math problem. It's a bit more complicated than that. I had a friend that might have been more, but that was long ago and he's forgotten about me."

"If you give me his name, I could look up his records. I could help you."

You wave a dismissive hand, "No, that's okay. I'm not sure what my 'correct path' is, but holding onto the past doesn't seem like a good answer either. I need a fresh start."

You put down your fork, your lunch only half finished. Looking at Eric, you take his hand, the warmth of it still a wonder. "I hate to see this end, but I think I need to stop pretending. Thank you, but do I need to drop you off somewhere or does your program just end or what?"

"I can be delivered back to my maker. The location is very close to your living quarters. Are you certain you wish to end the trial early? You haven't had a chance to explore all of my attributes fully. To experience love."

Your hair floats about your face as you shake your head. "Thanks, but no thanks. I think I'm ready to find something different. There's a million Davids out there who would love to help me experience love. No, that's not what I'm looking for."

Your path leads you back to where you started from. This time, on the monorail, you lean against Eric as you swing at the stops. The words of love on the wall advertisements don't stab into you. Love isn't something you get in a program or buy in a store. Love is something deeper.

The ease of your steps make the program worthwhile. This morning you had to force yourself to make each step, and now they come with an easy grace, accentuated by Eric's arm around your waist. He pulls you to a stop before a black door with the letters "C.W. Inc." on it.

He turns to you and puts his hands on each side of your face as he looks down at you.

"I need to ask again. Are you certain you want to end the trial early? I'm available for another 15 hours. If there's anything I can do for you, you need only ask."

You pull him towards you and give him a hug. He feels warm and real, but it's only an illusion. It's time you end all things from the surface.

"No, you did enough for me. Thanks. I think you helped me walk, but now it's time I learn to run on my own." You give him another brief kiss before he confirms your request and lifts his palm up to the door. A green scanner light hits his palm and then the door opens.

Eric turns back to you and extends his hand. "Please, this will just take a moment. They like to have the hand print to confirm the order cancellation and the satisfaction of the customer."

"You'd think they could do that from the phone app, but OK. I have the whole day off, after all."

You step over the threshold and into my world.

I can hear you now. Not through computer screens and enhancement tech, but here, right here, like I heard you so many years ago. Will you remember me? Or will I remain a spider hiding in the cobwebs of your memory?

"I will go to my compartment and ready myself for the next client. My maker is in the next room."

You named him Eric. My whole body halted as the words came out of your mouth. Did you know? But you didn't seem to realize what you had done. Still I was hopeful. After all, Eric is my name.

"Hello?"

I hear your tentative footsteps toward me. The click of your heels echoes in the silence of my technological cage. Now it's too late to go back. I can't wait any more. I've started and stopped too many times. I have to finish this now, even if it means revealing my broken body to you.

"I'm in here. Please come into my office." I call out to you, pleased that my voice doesn't sound as terrified as I feel.

One button makes my electric chair turn around to greet you as you walk into the room. The artificial limbs are hidden under a pleated pair of pants. Black dress shoes cover feet that are there for show. The freak genetic nature I was granted rejects most artificial adds. The flesh keeps failing as new neural connectors were sought. The result is, I have only partial movement in one arm. It's left me tied to the computer world after the accident.

Your eyes scan me over. Are you wondering if I'm human or is there another question in your mind that I don't know the answer to?

"Hello, Deirdre. I hope you found the trial to your satisfaction."

The silence stretches out as I focus on your face. Your brows push together and your nose flares ever so slightly as you try to figure out the puzzle before you.

"Eric? Eric Holden? Is that you? What... what happened?" The confusion seems mixed with concern, but you stop in the door. Not a step closer to the man before you.

"Yes, Dee, It's me. I never wanted you to see me like this. There was an auto accident after we moved. My parents... my parents didn't make it and I survived, but... well, there was permanent damage." My good arm directs a wave over the rest of my body.

One hand covers your mouth. Your black curls tumble around your shoulders as you shake your head in denial of my words. My friend, my dream. If I could only hold you

and make it all better, but I can't. I can't cross the divide that stretched out between us.

"An accident? You... you never... Why didn't you contact my family? Hell, Eric, we were best friends. What is this? You created this? You live two doors down from me but you never told me? Never reached out?"

You find a chair I had put by the door for other clients and fall into it. Your hands fully cover your face.

"Dee. I tried. I just couldn't."

How can I explain it to you? That the 13 year old boy you knew held on to the memory of you simply to survive? In the darkness of the recovery where everything I had known and loved was taken from me. When I have dreams, there is always Deirdre's face. Your face. Your hand stretches out to me as we run and tumble in the grass or lay on the floor, our computer screens so close they could be one and every now and then, you would lean your head against my shoulder.

You pull your hands away from your face. Red eyes greet me.

"Try... just try."

"I was 14, Dee. I was even hoping to visit you in the summer, when our car went off the road. I was in a coma for some time. The damage to my body was extensive. Weeks turned into months and then into years. I'm not a perfect match for the artificial connections. It took time. Lost time. By the time I finished school and found you again, you were established in your life. I didn't want to just break down your walls and intrude." The words sound like stupid excuses as I hear them come from my mouth. The real reason is, I was scared. Scared I would be rejected.

"Intrude on my life? So you created the Love app to say hello?"

You bite your lip as you wipe the tears from your eyes.

"Did you ever really think about me, Eric? What I might have really wanted? I went through my daily life not even knowing. Not knowing you were close. Not knowing you almost died. Not knowing anything. Were you watching me all this time? You're just... you're an idiot!"

You stand up suddenly and the chair falls over. I breathe in and close my eyes. Yes, I'm an idiot. An idiot to believe in what you were from my memories and not take into account what you became in the meantime. I've been cruel, using you in my own way. Using you to survive. I'll have to survive without you now. I wait for the click of your shoes to exit the room, but all I hear is our breathing.

"I'm sorry. I never wanted to hurt you. I wanted to help you. I still do. But I understand if you never want to see me again." My voice sounds as pitiful as my excuses.

"Do you think I'm that shallow?"

I hear movement and open my eyes again. You had turned to face me. Your eyes take me in with an intensity I haven't seen before.

"No, Dee, I never thought you were shallow."

"I'm probably an idiot, too. I never tried to find you. I just went on with my life and wrote you off as *what might have been.* I want to believe in the things I talked with Eric about. I think love isn't something just physical, or it shouldn't be if it's going to last. And I want it to last. I'm tired of running."

You step closer to my chair. So close that I smell you. I don't dare to speak.

"I want that friendship again. I don't want all these computer screens and AI's between us."

Then I feel the touch of your hand on my good hand. For the first time, my wall crumples. You are real, truly

real, instead of an anchor that a sick boy holds onto to survive. For that moment we are two 13-year-olds again at the dance. This time, though, I won't let go.

"I'd like that too, Dee. No more hiding, OK?"

"Yes, no more hiding. And you have to tell me everything, and I mean everything." The harsh tone of voice is lessened by the smile on your lips.

With great effort, I manage to squeeze your hand. Whatever I have to reveal will be worth it. You've entered my life again and I'm willing to pay that price for a second chance. A start of a new life with whatever years I have left.

Always Something

Keith Ellis

Keith Ellis is a local writer and smart-ass who went to grad school at the University of Washington and has worked as a Trade Magazine Publisher. He is too good to write his own bio and is not really all that frightened of birds. Promise.

You can tell a lot about a man by how he treats the woman he's with. Whether he pays attention to her, whether he caters to her interests, or just uses her as a prop or an ego boost. If the latter, he might be in trouble.

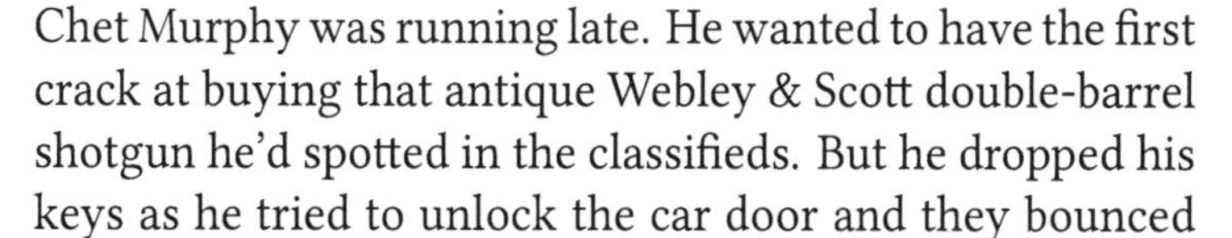

Chet Murphy was running late. He wanted to have the first crack at buying that antique Webley & Scott double-barrel shotgun he'd spotted in the classifieds. But he dropped his keys as he tried to unlock the car door and they bounced under the vehicle.

"Naturally," he fumed. In Murphy's view of the cosmos, the powers-that-be were out to ruin his life with itty-bitty mishaps, a constant flow of minor irritants that would keep him from ever achieving happiness. He had to lie on his belly with stick in hand to reach the keys.

Of course, the branch snapped. He responded, as usual, with a stream of profanities. He found a stouter twig and hooked the errant keys. He had to go back inside and change his dirty shirt, putting him even more behind in his race for the prized shotgun. That's me, he thought, a day late and a dollar short. He was agitated for the entire drive to Camano Island.

He'd driven 45 minutes to the bridge and another half hour to the tip of the island, only to find out that while the gun was still available, its stock was marred with scratches. Although the gun was in otherwise excellent condition, at a price much less than Murphy was prepared to pay had the weapon been pristine, he demurred curtly and was unceremoniously on his way.

He was disappointed, but then disappointment was Murphy's frequent companion. There was always something. Besides, he already owned the serviceable shotgun he kept in his living room. So he was driving normally and, sure, he'd spotted the trio of crows three hundred yards away, bouncing around some hapless road-kill, each vying for the choicest cut of the flattened opossum, and no, he hadn't reduced his speed.

They were crows. He couldn't run them over even if he wanted to; they were too cautious, too damn smart to be caught with their tail-feathers down.

The three birds took flight as Murphy approached their picnic. Then one, after flying just a few feet, unexpectedly dropped back down to the blacktop and returned to the feast. Murphy couldn't stop in time and so he didn't attempt to brake. He watched the crow's carcass in his rearview mirror, spinning like the top half of a baseball bat that had been broken off by a fastball. The bird rolled to the side of the road. It was dead, run over. Murphy took no pleasure in the death of anything.

Still, it was out of his mind, more or less, by the next bend in the road.

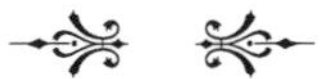

A few days later, Chet Murphy was again in his usual emotional state: peeved. Some fool was tapping on the colored window alongside his front door instead of using the damn doorbell. He'd put that plate of glass in just the week before and he'd scraped his hand doing it. That moron should at least knock on the door if pressing the ringer is so difficult.

His irritation rose with each tap. He glanced at the shotgun leaning against his fireplace to reassure himself. Lots of crazies out there. He stood, threw his newspaper into the seat of the chair and stalked towards the door. He yanked it open.

A woman stood sideways to the door so that he saw only her profile. She tilted her chin up towards him, pushing a lock of lush black hair from her brow with her slender fingers as she studied him with a single doe eye.

"Mr. Murphy?" she asked.

He stared back at her with a hedged expression that could have meant either "Who wants to know?" or "Never heard of him." She asked again.

"Mr. Chet Murphy?"

Her unblemished skin was tinted olive. She had shoulder-length black hair, full sensual lips. She was small, petite even, yet curvy: voluptuousness scaled down. Her ample chest was close to disproportionate, an unbalance Murphy found compelling. (On the other hand, he thought her beret was stupid—but, then, there's always something.) Under the onslaught of her beauty, his righteous indignation streamed out of him, the urge to slam the door in her face dissipated. She was, as a mobster in a 1930's movie might say, a frail. Vulnerable, needing protection – needing, perhaps, Chet Murphy.

"How may I help you?" he asked, neither confirming nor denying his identity.

Her right hand began to move towards him and he saw she was holding a business card.

"I'm Carin Corvus," she said. "I'm with the Bird Sanctuary of Camano Island."

He took the card and noted the stylized black bird in one corner. Her title identified her as the owner. He relaxed some. Murphy was educated enough and well-read enough and pragmatic enough to embrace a certain amount of tree-huggery, as long as it wasn't overboard.

"Are you seeking donations?" he asked, thinking he might part with a ten-spot and ask her in for coffee.

"Actually, Mr. Murphy," she replied, her voice soft yet determined, "I was wondering how you could run over one of our crows and just drive off as if nothing happened."

Murphy was taken aback. He placed his right hand upon his chest, ready to protest, about to deny involvement in any bird's death, when he remembered. He had been the cause of a crow's demise. He flipped her business card in his fingers, feeling the bite of its hard edges.

"You mean that crow on Camano Island..." He shrugged.

"He had a name, you know," she replied. "Oscar."

Rain began to fall. Carin's expression softened. "I guess you wouldn't know. I'm an ornithologist. We've been studying corvid intelligence at the Bird Sanctuary. Oscar was one of our more interesting... participants." Drops made tiny rivulets down the young woman's face

that were not caused, as Murphy hoped, by weather overspray. "It's hard not to become attached."

"Please," Murphy said as the drizzle became a pour, "come in. Let me take your coat. I can have a pot of coffee on before you know it."

She stepped inside, removing her jacket and, as Murphy would come to describe it, her god-awful beret, and sat at his kitchenette. Murphy began to recite the specifics of Oscar's death, but Carin cut him off: she'd seen the whole thing. She'd even jotted down his license number and had a "friend of the sanctuary" run his plates at the Department of Licensing to find his address. He didn't trust the government any more than the cosmos. He mentally filed that grievance against her for later.

"I'm really very sorry," he said, trying to wrap the subject up. "I've never seen a crow do anything so stupid."

She cocked her head. "Oscar wasn't stupid," she said. "He was greedy, always trying to get more than his share."

"Sounds like a lot of people I know," Murphy said.

"That's why they fascinate me." Carin became animated. "Their brains are so different from ours, I mean, anatomically speaking, yet all the human emotions seem to be there, the good and the bad."

They spoke about the young woman's work, a conversation in which both hungrily engaged. For different reasons, they had each isolated themselves from much in the way of spirited discourse. Murphy perceived her as a kindred spirit: intelligent, passionate, attractive. A person, he surmised, that appreciated her own company. He could envision a well-worn copy of *Atlas Shrugged* on her nightstand. They made a coffee date for the following Saturday as they walked to her Volkswagen Bug.

"I guess I could use a break." Her small smile seemed to signal hope, the wish for a sanctuary from her sorrow granted. Murphy, in turn, hoped it would be the first step toward observing her disrobed. Beyond that, he was already quite infatuated. She drove off as he wondered what would screw this up for him.

There's always something. Murphy kicked at a pebble at the thought, a pebble that decided to veer off toward his front door and put a visible crack in his new window.

All the glib remarks Murphy had dreamed up during the trip to the island for their date abandoned him as he waited outside the coffee shop and saw her walking to meet him.

"I'm glad you could make it," was all he could manage to say. He didn't realize how broadly he was smiling until he saw the hint of surprise in her eyes and her own wide grin.

"Let's sit there," she said, pointing at a booth on the other side of the glass. "It's nippy out here. The sun will feel good through the window."

He held the door for her, then helped her off with her jacket. She took off her beret (*Thankfully*, thought Murphy) and sat down.

"Latte?" he asked.

"Mocha. Double-shot, please."

He went to the counter and bought her the rich drink—the whipped cream was his idea—and a regular coffee for himself. He sat down with both forearms on the table so that he could warm his hands on his cup. She cocked her head to examine his drink. She touched his wrist.

"No foo-foo drinks for you, I see," she said.

His cheeks colored from the light pressure of her hand on his arm.

"Lattes give me a headache."

"Paying four dollars for coffee gives me a headache," she said. "Thanks for the treat." Her eyes smiled at him over the rim of the cup as she took her first sip. "Mmmm. I love whipped cream."

Her approval made him laugh and she echoed him, throwing back her head a bit and exposing her long, lovely neck. She used both hands to pull her hair back over her shoulders. His tension evaporated and was replaced with an inner vibration: a full-body tingling that would revisit him whenever she was near. He asked about the crows and the ensuing conversation lasted until both their cups were cold and the barista was shooting them the occasional it's-closing-time glance.

On their second date, they did what all young lovers in the area do: took the hour ride on the ferry from Seattle to Bremerton. They sat across from each other on the cot-sized green vinyl benches—their relationship too new to sit shoulder-to-shoulder, thigh to thigh—and looked at the various islands that broke the dark expanse of water. Though it was midday, the sky was overcast. The peaks of land in the distance were gray and a light rain pelted the picture windows that lined the passenger deck.

Murphy wondered if it was the thrum of the ship's huge engines he felt, or his own body's reaction to Carin's proximity. He asked her if she could feel the vibration, subconsciously hoping she would say, "Is that what it is? I thought I was in love."

She winked, which to Murphy was close enough, then stood to press her palms against the observational plate glass between them and the sea. Something caught her eye and she moved several benches down for a better look.

He watched her walking away, focusing, as he did at every opportunity, on her gait, the wide side-to-side swing of her backside. It was nearly a caricature of a woman's walk and it fascinated Murphy.

Carin didn't seem to notice when he joined her at the window, so intent on the seabird that paced the ferry and appeared to hover just on the other side of the glass, but then she spoke to him.

"That's a California Gull. Larus californicus. Its ancestors saved some Mormon settlers from a grasshopper plague in 1848." She pointed at a large gull that had landed on the deck outside of their window. "See that one there? The mottled gray one? That's a Glaucous-Wing. They turn mostly white when they get older."

"Ah, a woman of many disciplines." Murphy exploited the chance to draw her into conversation. "You study seagulls, too?"

"Had to," she answered. "They're bad to my boys."

Inspired, Murphy asked, "What's black and white and rolls around the parking lot?" He didn't give her time to answer. "A crow and a seagull fighting over a french fry."

The ferry had steamed under a dark, swollen cloud that blotted out much of the light. A dirty gray cast mottled the sky and large drops of rain smacked into the windows like mud splattering against a wall. The black weather curtained the scenery so Murphy turned his focus to Carin. She was facing him but her attention was still upon the window, peering at it sideways.

Murphy needed to fill the void. "Of course, the crow wins." She seemed not to hear, turning to face the window. Murphy pressed on. "The french fry, I mean."

A slap against the pane rang so loudly his head swiveled instantly toward the glass. A large gull had

smashed into the top of the window with such force that its beak had broken nearly off. Blood oozed from the tear and the bird's body, perhaps suctioned on by rivulets of rain, clung to the porthole. Wings spread wide, it resembled a feathered crucifix. It began to slide down, streaks of crimson dividing the window like a white stripe parts a highway. Random tufts of down decorated the hemoglobin line.

The bird still lived. Murphy thought he could read its eye: Neither pain nor fear, but hate. It seemed to stare straight at Carin as it continued its gelatinous movement down. Murphy looked to her, expecting an expression of horror, but she merely stared back at the gull, her pupils narrowed to the size of pinpricks.

The ferry jolted against a wave and the fowl dropped from the window, bounced off the outside sill and disappeared into the abyss of turbulent brine.

"That poor bastard," he said. He shook his head.

Her red-painted lips were momentarily pursed into a rose bud. She shrugged.

"Don't waste your sympathy," she said. "It was brain-dead when it hatched."

It only happened the one time, during Carin's first night as his live-in girlfriend. She arose because she'd left her backpack in the Volkswagen.

"Don't get up," she said. "It'll only take a minute."

He lay on his back, his arm bent under his head. He heard tapping on his window, thought of the first time he had met Carin, and decided it must be her. Irritated, he got up, went to the sound and pulled back the curtain.

The crow opposite him was as startled as Murphy. The big bird froze, its head cocked to the side, too surprised to take flight. They eyed each other, inches apart, only a thin sheet of glass between them. Finally the crow dropped something from its beak, a little nondescript ball that reflected the moonlight, before quickly snatching it back up. In a flurry and rattle of feathers, it disappeared into the night.

Carin came into the bedroom shortly after, moved some of the items from her knapsack into her side of the dresser, and slid into bed. Murphy briefly wondered if visiting crows would be the something that ruined his romance. But there were no more late night sightings and gradually the incident faded from his memory, reoccurring only one more time when, as he snooped through Carin's drawers, he found a wadded-up foil from a cigarette package.

The air had a chill to it when they met at the Island Coffee Shop, but the trees were greening. Instead of heavy winter coats, the couple both wore wind breakers. It had been six months since their first date that past fall and they had come back for caffeine many times. The barista knew them both by name and brought Murphy his coffee and Carin her mocha without being asked. Carin looked down at her drink as she stirred in the whipped cream.

"Is it the Beret thing?" Murphy asked. "All I meant was that it's about 40 years out of date, okay? But if you want to wear it, I'm fine with that."

He'd made a joke about beatniks when she had last worn the cap. She'd been downbeat ever since and now she was having second thoughts about their living arrangement.

"It's the commute, I guess," she said. "It's starting to wear me down."

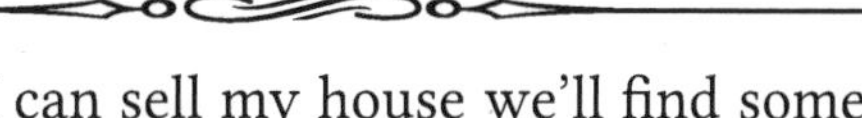

"As soon as I can sell my house we'll find somewhere closer," he lied. He knew she'd get used to the drive. Besides, she wasn't going to be studying birds forever.

"Really?" She looked up. "That would be great."

Their courtship had gone smoother than Murphy had hoped. He kept waiting for something to come along and suck the happiness out of him, but it hadn't. Last February he'd talked her into moving into his house. He thought their relationship was maturing at a good pace.

Sure, Murphy thought, there were some cracks in the paint. For one thing, her bosom was more chest than breast and her legs were skinny, but she was still a ten. OK, an eight-and-a-half. Her sense of humor also left something to be desired: couldn't she take a little joke about her stupid hat? Still, he knew he would be happy with her as his life's partner. She might seem tentative about their future at the moment, but Murphy had learned that he could charm her into seeing things his way.

"Tell you what," he said. "I'll buy the fixings for dinner on my way home. It'll be hot on the table when you get there at six. How's that sound?"

She cocked her head and looked at him from the side. He knew he had her interest when she did that.

"That sounds good," she said. "I'm sorry about being a baby."

"Just as long as you're my baby," he said, patting her hand. "I'll go to the store right now."

She allowed him to peck her lips, but stayed in her chair as he walked into the parking lot. Murphy waved goodbye.

He was thinking about her as he wandered the aisles at the grocery store. He picked out some frozen sweet corn still on the cob and selected one of the pricier Merlots the store had to offer. On his mind was the expensive necklace he'd bought her, the one she only wore when he reminded her of it. Funny, when they were first dating he'd strung together a handful of pop tops from soda cans on an elastic band and presented it to her with exaggerated pomp and circumstance. She had loved the trinket. At first he thought she was being sarcastic, just going along with the joke, but she wore Murphy's gift either on her wrist or ankle nearly every day.

"It's so shiny," she'd said.

He thought he'd make points with her with real jewelry and had sprung for the necklace; a jade crow, stylized in the manner of Native American art and set in gray pewter. Yet he could tell from her eyes that she didn't much care for it. It stayed in her drawer much of the time. Women, he thought, who knows what they want.

Murphy set to cooking as soon as he returned home. He broiled pork ribs, warmed up some rice and cooked the ears of corn. He pulled open his cutlery door and was surprised to find his cork screw missing. It was a chrome job he'd picked up at a men's store years before he'd met Carin; it still gleamed as if new and its look was modern in design. There's always something, Murphy thought, as he looked over the kitchen table and counter-tops. The gadget was gone. He swore a bit, then dug through the spoons, forks and knives until he found his old bottle opener. It worked well enough but Murphy remained miffed at the universe until he heard Carin's Volkswagon rumble into the driveway.

He watched her settle in front of her plate of food, hoping her mood had changed since he saw her last. Carin seemed to welcome the ready-made meal. She poked holders into the ends of the corn, picked it up an inch from the plate, then bent her head down to nip off a few kernels at a time.

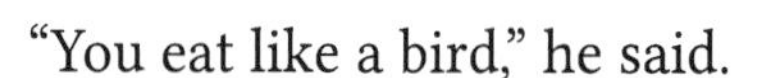

"You eat like a bird," he said.

"Most people ask me if I have a hollow leg," she said, smiling. It was true; the girl had a healthy appetite.

"No, I mean you eat like a bird," he said. He smiled, too, but only with his lips. "Why don't you bring the corn up to your mouth like the rest of us humans?"

She rested the corn on her plate and looked at him squarely with the same pained look she'd had when he'd remarked on her beret.

"I've had enough," she said.

"You've only had a few bites."

"No, I've had enough of you and your comments," she said. She got up and fled into their room. Murphy remained, muttering. He ate some, gave it up, and went to his easy chair. He started polishing his shotgun, not because it needed it, but because he was trying not to give in to a tantrum by following her.

He heard something hit their bed and the springs creak. He rose, still cradling the gun in the crook of his arm and entered the room. An open suitcase lay on the mattress and she was throwing clothes into it. She looked up at him and stood still, her head cocked and her closest eye concentrated on the gun. He noticed her fear, decided it was to his advantage, and casually kept the barrels of the piece pointed in her direction.

"Aren't you overreacting?" he asked, rubbing the gun with the rag. "I was just kidding."

After a pause she said, "Yeah. You're right. I'm tired, I guess. Mind if I just go to bed?"

"Sure, sure," he said. "I'll put the dishes away and join you. You'll feel better in the morning."

She took her eye from the gun and looked at his face.

"I will," she said. "I know I will."

She was asleep when he climbed in beside her and did not rouse when he ran his hand along the curves of her waist and hips. She'll be okay by tomorrow. He turned his back to her and soon lightly snored. Carin slid out of the bed and quietly left the room.

Murphy woke around 10 am and did not feel her back against his. The spring sun lit the room even through the shades. Carin had hastily placed the still-opened suitcase on the only chair in the room before going to bed. It wasn't unpacked. After checking to see if the bedroom door was fully closed, he rummaged through it. Underclothes seemed to be as far as she got, but then a gleam caught his eye. It was his missing corkscrew.

"What the..." he said aloud. He felt around and found more shiny things: A new dime, a tiny, pot-metal heart—probably a piece from a cheap charm bracelet—and a wadded-up strip of aluminum foil. He studied the bright ball in his hand, and then tossed it back into the luggage. He strode to their shared dresser, opened the top drawer and took out a small, felt box. There, inside, lay the jade crow. Foil made the cut, he thought, but not a $350.00 necklace.

He called her name. No answer. He hurriedly pulled the shades and saw that her car was still in the drive. He looked to the yard but saw no sign of her and was about to close the blinds when some movement caught the corner of his eye.

It was a crow—hell, one of the biggest crows he'd ever seen. No, it wasn't a raven. It didn't have the wedge-shaped tail of a raven; its tail was the fan-shape of a crow—Carin had taught him that much, at least. This thing looked more like a big black chicken than a wild bird. It was hopping around oddly. Murphy knitted his brows as he watched, then he saw the problem. The bird had Carin's soda top bracelet; the one Murphy had made for her. Somehow it had wrapped around the bird's neck and one of its wings. Murphy didn't think it could fly.

He watched it stop hopping and start the stiff-legged march of its kind. It made Murphy think back to that time on the ferry when he'd first noticed how Carin's posterior swung so much. Man, Murphy thought, she's been with those birds too long; she's becoming one of them.

He stiffened at the thought and his eyes grew round. The huge crow suddenly cocked its head to look, one-eyed, at something in the dirt.

That's when he knew.

That's when he knew that something was going to take all the happiness he had known since meeting the love of his life and grind it into his face, squash it into his being. This wasn't a little something, like most of the spitballs thrown at him by the gods. This was the mother of all somethings.

He compiled a list of evidence in a flash of insight. He remembered her eating the corn the night before. He thought of her name, how obvious was that? She'd been stealing shiny things like a magpie: the corkscrew, the foil, shiny things like that stupid bracelet she had around her neck that very minute.

She wasn't an expert on crows; she was the queen of the fricking crows. The bitch was getting revenge, lifting him up to throw him down because he'd accidentally—accidentally, mind you—run over one of her "boys."

He threw on his pants, jammed his feet into slippers, and crept out into the yard. The fat, black fowl that was most certainly Carin hadn't noticed him; she was still trying to untangle herself from the bracelet. He held his breath, moving slowly, getting closer until he was able to dart out his right arm and swoop this dodo of a crow up.

He caught her, held her up over his head and screamed at the frightened, cawing bird.

"I'm going to kill you, Carin," he yelled. "You are not getting over on me, damn you."

Sergeant Dusty Cromwell propped himself up, his clammy hand pressed against the Plexiglas that paralleled the front door. He'd seen death in many forms during his two decades with the police force: the freshly killed, the thoroughly decomposed and, yes, bodies picked over by the resident fauna. He thought himself immune to the nausea brought on by a scene of carnage. But a glimpse of that huge crow before it propelled itself into the air, its head sticky with gore, and the empty, bloody eye-sockets of the deceased's still-warm body, unearthed sensibilities Cromwell thought long buried. "Damn crows will eat anything," he thought. Even as he fought the bile burning in the base of his throat, he wondered how it had come to this for the person whose torn body lay mere feet from the front porch. Then again, there was always something.

Carin told Cromwell that the shotgun had just gone off. She'd heard Murphy ranting in the front yard and fear forced her to grab the weapon. Her lover's back was still towards her when the gun seemed to buck of its own accord. The blast tore off the section of Murphy's waist where his love handle had been. Carin saw the wound appear as if a huge, invisible carnivore had taken a bite from Murphy's side.

But Murphy was still alive when the buckshot spun him around, fully conscious when he saw his sweet girlfriend again raise the shotgun and blast a hole clean through his chest. The crow he held, now free from the bracelet an angry Carin had thrown out the window the previous night, flew into a nearby tree. Murphy fell face-down into the dew-laden grass. Carin told Cromwell that she mistook the crow for a handgun, that her second shot was intentional, that it was self-defense.

Cromwell overrode his desire to vomit and pushed himself away from Murphy's ornate window. He looked at the oddly-shaped woman, her top heavy and her legs spindly, as she sat on the porch and sobbed into her hands. He bent down and lightly encircled her upper arm with his fingers and said, "Let's go."

He neither handcuffed her, nor made her ride in the backseat. He'd never been gentler with a murderer.

Carin sold the land of her bird sanctuary to cover the cost of her defense. Her attorney had wrapped up their case neatly in his closing arguments.

"You've listened to the testimony of James Baker," he told the jury. "You've listened to the testimony of Marius Carstesen and Ann Rondell, neighbors all of Chet Murphy and Carin Corvus. They heard what my client heard. Chet Murphy said he was going to kill Carin Corvus. And so she armed herself, armed herself with the very shotgun Chet Murphy had once pointed at her.

"Carin has admitted that the first shot was an accident. The prosecution has not offered any proof that she was the least bit familiar with firearms. But when Chet Murphy turned around, brandishing a dark shape that for all the world looked like a gun... Well, ladies and gentlemen, put yourself in Carin's position. You've heard testimony of Chet Murphy's verbal abuse, his fits of rage. He's just been threatening to kill you and it appears as if he is holding a weapon. If you can put yourself in the scene, you can understand that for all intents and purposes it was a situation of kill or be killed. If you can

understand that, you must return a verdict of not guilty to the charge of murder for Carin Corvus."

And they did. Not guilty of murder, but guilty of the lesser charge of manslaughter. She was sentenced to time served (six months) and 15 months of outpatient therapy.

On the final day of treatment, Carin left the office of the psychologist and walked to the bus stop. She no longer rued the selling of her beloved Volkswagen; it was just one more bad thing in a long list of bad things. A soft breeze engaged her bangs in a dance. She stretched her arms out from her sides and—for the first time since Oscar had died, for the first time since Chet Murphy had come into her life—flew.

Love Lost in Limbo

Lance Browne

Lance Browne grew up in Eastern Washington State farmland. This gave him lots of time to read. He read about other worlds, other times and wondered what was possible or "impossible" that might be possible. Ideas that always mutated with the next book. This story is another possibility.

Love is blind and sometimes it takes a lot, when we're in love, to see the objects of our affection as they truly are. It can take time, or it can take an extremely traumatic event to bring us perspective.

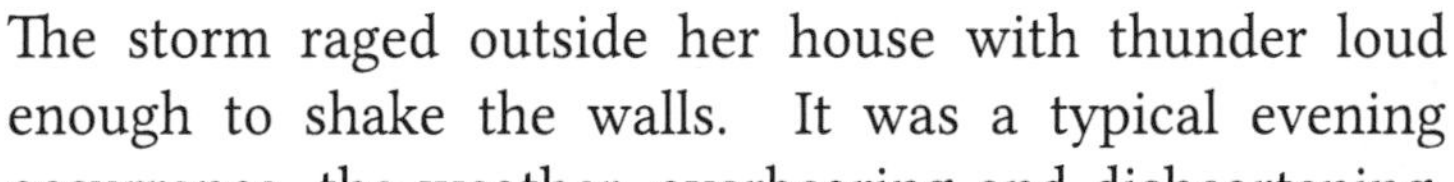

The storm raged outside her house with thunder loud enough to shake the walls. It was a typical evening occurrence, the weather, overbearing and disheartening, incessantly nudging some of the easily susceptible into acting rashly.

Donna watched it rage through the house's windows. She had come to appreciate the storms, trying to imagine the amount of energy required to create the nightly show, marveling at the spectacle. Safe inside her place, a veritable bubble of protection, it was much different than being outside in the storm. Tonight would not be a good night to be outside, she thought to herself.

Inspired by this show of wild power, she turned back to her current passion: painting. She was very good at it. All of her clients were extremely happy with the paintings she had made for them. Her latest one was for Melvin and she was focused on ensuring that all the details were as perfect as she could make them. She wanted him to love it. She knew a lot about Melvin; his coworkers that she had met never stopped saying nice things about him. He deserved nothing less than her best and she was going to give it to him.

Melvin's primary interests were his family and his work, so Donna had decided to incorporate both into the painting. Before she started on it, she researched what his dream home would be and what his family looked like. She drew multiple sketches of each person to ensure the best representation of each, which was needed with Melvin's mind sometimes slipping. Now it was up to her to add the emotions of happiness and wonder to the people he remembered so fondly.

She studied the painting in front of her, analyzing each person to ensure they were all exuding a sense of family bonding during a holiday dinner. She felt growing excitement that this was going to be her best painting yet, capturing a perfect balance of nostalgia and polish. Satisfied with the facial features and expressions, she changed her focus and started double-checking the angles of the bodies and eyes. She made sure that the parents were positioned correctly for fondly overlooking their children and the kids were looking at all the food on the table as if determining what to eat first. (Although one nephew of Melvin's was obviously contemplating something mischievous.) With nothing out of place, she was satisfied that it was ready for the him to see.

While waiting for her client to drop by, she found herself thinking of John, her fiancé. He was the real reason she desperately wanted Melvin to appreciate the painting: whatever it took to bring her one step closer to reuniting with him. She had mixed emotions thinking of John, unsure how such a reunion would play out. She had trouble understanding what was going on in their relationship, not knowing if John liked things how they were or if she needed to change something to make John happier.

Finally, she heard Melvin enter her house and prepared to wait while he got comfortable coming in from the miserable outside weather.

Melvin hung up his coat on the rack near the door like he did every time he came by. He smiled and nodded at Donna, telling her he made it to her place, but had to sit a spell and watch some TV to recover from the cold. Donna nodded, asking if she could get him something to eat or drink, knowing he would refuse. Melvin started clicking through the channels until it seemed he had checked every one several times, but nothing caught his interest and so he turned it off. He sat staring at the blank screen a moment and then said as if to himself, "There never seems to be anything on that catches my interest anymore." He added in an even lower voice, "Just as well."

Speaking up, he said, "Just to let you know, I think work is going well, at least it looks like the building will be ready for the grand opening soon. Not sure how that is, since so many folks seem to be missing. Even one of my best friends quit. James. Found that out just the other day. I thought James would never leave before the building was done. Strange, that. Same for a few others, now that I think about it."

Melvin paused, mulling it over. "I wonder why they left – if they found better jobs..." He stared off in silence. "... or new dreams to follow. I hope so. I would want them moving on to a better life."

Donna thought about James and some of the other guys and hoped Melvin was right about them moving on to a better life. "I am sure James and anyone else you are wondering about are doing better now, and if they aren't..." She paused and then concluded, "Well, I just hope they are doing better. I like to believe that's true."

Melvin bobbed his head a few times and continued staring at the TV, as if it was a fireplace giving warmth in a cold room. "Did I ever tell you how I got into the construction business?" He spoke as if reminiscing, rather than asking a question.

She answered anyway, glad to encourage the story: "Why did you?"

"I always wanted to be an architect. I remember as a kid I would build all kinds of things with Legos and I always wondered what it would be like to do it for real. My parents were happy I enjoyed the toys; but to me, in my mind I was building libraries, hotels, even skyscrapers. I eventually started drawing plans and then I'd spend hours trying to create buildings based on my plans with Legos." Laughing, he added, "It's funny how much you can learn about understanding building plans when you put the plastic to them."

He paused again, staring at the TV out of habit since it was off and after a moment, he continued, "That was the dream when I was young – to be an architect. I failed because I couldn't pass the math classes to get the degree. How does math or a degree prove you have imagination?

If anything, all a degree proves is accepted standards have been drilled into your head. Some things just don't make sense."

After a moment, he continued, "So construction it was; closest I could get to being an architect. It was the best decision I ever made. I met my wife at my first construction job and I soon realized that creating the buildings was what I enjoyed more than the designing. After all, that's really what I was doing with the Legos: building. It took a while, but it dawned on me that when I tried to build something based on my plans it never worked and I would always finish by ignoring them."

Wanting to confirm her suspicion, Donna asked, "So you're happy how things turned out?"

Melvin startled, like he'd forgotten she was there. He probably had, she mused. "Absolutely! When I think of my family and friends and all the fun times... I wouldn't want it any other way." He had a smile on his face when he turned to look at her, showing her he really meant it.

The answer made Donna happy. "Want to look at what I've painted for you?"

Melvin came to look and stopped part way there. "Did you paint those buildings from what we talked about? I always wanted to build a house like that to live in. That family is lucky to live in a grand place like that."

After staring at the house for a while, he came closer and started to look at the people seated at an outdoor table and gasped. "You painted my Matilda next to the only empty chair. She looks radiant like she always does." He scanned the faces some more. "This painting is like a photograph of a family reunion we never had."

"Do you think I should paint you into the empty chair?" she asked.

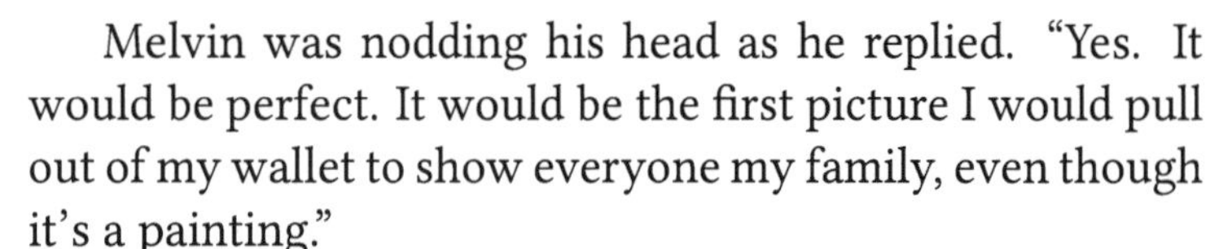

Melvin was nodding his head as he replied. "Yes. It would be perfect. It would be the first picture I would pull out of my wallet to show everyone my family, even though it's a painting."

"That's nice of you to say, but adding your ugly mug to the painting might ruin it." She laughed as she said it and stopped herself from hugging him and looked at him to be sure he knew she meant it in a positive way and added, "Take care on your walk home tonight. Thanks for everything and have sweet dreams."

He smiled at her joke and sentiment, "Thanks, Donna. I'm sure I will. Have a good night."

Donna was glad that she was able to respond in a cheerful voice, "You can come by and pick the painting up sometime next week." She closed her eyes and reminded herself of her goals.

The sounds from the storm or whatever it was paused the next day, allowing her to become slowly reacquainted with silence, impressing upon her how enjoyable peace and quiet could be. With the bombardment of eerie sounds at a halt, she was amazed at how the calm made her want to leave to a different place where it was always peaceful, although she knew she couldn't do that without Sam's approval. She wasn't sure how she knew, but after thinking of him, she could tell he had arrived for their daily discussions. "Hello, Sam."

He slowly came into the room and responded, "Always with the name."

"Well, it makes things seem more normal to me. Which is important, since "normalness" is hard to come by here with no family and friends to see, no going out for dinner, no driving a car, no shopping, no anything." She looked

at Sam, wanting him to grant a reprieve but knowing it wouldn't happen.

"Regarding your desire to leave, as we discussed before, all you have to do is give up on John. What was John to you, anyways? Don't you want to move where it can be silent and enjoyable? Aren't you ready to leave?"

"No," was the answer she always gave. She wasn't sure why they kept trying to make her give up on John, but if she could have John and everything she wanted with extra work, she was going to work.

"Well, let's go to my office and we shall discuss this some more." As always, they left her comfort zone and went to Sam's area, which was always set up with temptations to make her give up and stop trying to win her way back to John.

Sam indicated she should sit in her chair and get as comfortable as she could. "So how is the food at your place? I ask because we have set up this special table of enticements for you." Sam did something and a curtain fell, exposing all the food that her imagination had conjured up. The aromas weren't make-believe – they were real, from all the food on the table in front of her. Then a fan was turned on in case she wasn't smelling the food enough already. She inhaled deeply and detected bacon, coffee, several spices and even some fresh fruits. She looked longingly at the chocolate cake and candies, trying to detect the subtle smell of chocolate that was hidden by the other aromas.

Donna stopped paying attention to the food when she heard Sam ask her, "Remember what eating this food was like? Let me know when you're ready to enjoy it all again." She remained quiet, wondering if she was getting close to capitulating.

Sam asked her to turn her chair to look at the other direction and while she was doing that, Sam started the videos stretching across the walls. The videos were showing her life back home, what she could be part of if she turned on John. Her friends and relatives were living life as one would expect, not knowing her current situation. The thought of returning to them was the hardest to resist. She watched and was pulled into how normal their lives seemed, going to school, driving to work, eating out (especially after watching the table of food), even shopping. Her aunt was shopping in a department store, trying on shoes with a jewelry and cosmetic counter visible behind her. She wondered if her aunt was really going to buy all the items the video showed her with or if the video was staged with enticing embellishment.

After a while, what she was watching switched to display other scenes she could easily imagine herself enjoying. One of her favorites consisted of a beach with nothing on it, just the surf rolling in and out and an occasional gull flying by. It seemed so peaceful.

Donna sat through the remaining time of temptations without saying anything. For now, she was safe, but she wondered how long her resolution to get back to her fiancé would last.

Donna thought about Melvin and wondered if he would be returning or if someone new would come to her place that night that she would have to paint for.

Of all the people it could have been, she didn't expect her fiancé to come through the door. When she saw him, she ran into his arms and hugged him, giddy with joy. "John! I can't believe it's you!" As she was hugging him, she was aware something was off, but she chose to ignore the thought and just enjoy being with him. Her fiancé was here! It was time for them to go home! Sam and his group must have given up!

"Where am I? That thunder sounds really loud." John spoke in a frightened voice as he disentangled himself from her hugs.

"What?" Donna asked in a puzzled voice. "Oh, the thunder! You hear the thunder? In fact..." She started to think about what it meant for John to be with her, where she was. "What are you doing here? Did you get hurt?" She blurted out the questions, when all she really wanted was to do was just hold him.

"Wait—you're awake and walking around? Don't take this wrong, I am glad you're doing well, but none of this makes sense." He moved away from Donna to try and figure out his situation.

"John, if you're here, something must have happened." She didn't want to think about it. A small part of her wondered if it might all be a ruse by Sam and his group with someone that looked like John, but whoever it was, he looked like John so she went with it. "What do you remember last?" she asked, afraid to hear his answer.

"I remember meeting Benny—he was the guy who hooked me up on how to make some money. It was going to be how we started our new life. The last thing Benny told me was that the boss man with the money was in the back room." John looked around like the door to the back room was nearby. "If I can just see the boss man and get my money." He looked at Donna and frowned, "I mean our money, honey. It was going to be okay, but then you got hit and went into a coma. Umm, I don't feel well and I don't understand what's going on." Looking around, he noticed his surroundings for the first time. "How did we get back to our old apartment? I left that place as soon I could after you got hit."

Donna didn't understand what her fiancé was saying about money, or who Benny or boss man was, and could only respond with what she understood: "You left our apartment?"

He turned and looked at her, "I hated that place. That's why I hooked up with Benny. To make money to get out of there. He told me there was a group who would pay to have the construction site suffer a setback, the longer the setback the bigger the payout. I worked hard to ensure a nice payout. We were going to move with that money. Then I forgot my lunch and you had to bring it to me at work. I wasn't thinking about lunch that day. I never imagined you would get hurt in the accident."

She stared at John and didn't know what to say.

"Yeah, not proud of it, but the payout was for a lot of money. I didn't mean for anyone to get hurt." He looked at her for understanding and didn't see any. Frustrated, he said, "I need to find Benny and get away from this annoying noise. It's driving me crazy."

He started walking to the door when Donna grabbed his arm to hold him from leaving and she said, "Don't go. Please stay here."

Shaking his head, he said, "I have to find Benny, meet with the boss man, get my money, and then we can move wherever we want to. You always wanted to travel, didn't you? Look, I'll figure this all out." This time, he slipped out of Donna's grasp and left.

Devastated, Donna started crying, not believing what she had just heard. All this time fighting to save John and he walked out.

She was hoping Sam would show up to tell her what it meant that John was here. Was there no more deal to be made? As the thoughts were mulling around in her mind, John came back in.

John was smiling as he hugged her and said, "It's okay. I've got it all straightened out. You just need to paint a picture of someplace where we dreamed of living and then we can live there and enjoy ourselves. They told me you're a great painter now." He looked at her, trying to figure out when she learned to paint and what else she was hiding from him. Then he added, to ensure she understood what he wanted, "Remember we always talked about moving to Vegas. Getting a penthouse suite when we could afford it. Well now we can afford it!"

She heard what he said but felt that there must be sound waves distorting the words. He couldn't really believe what he was staying, she thought. She collected her thoughts and tried to explain the situation to John. "It won't work, John. The paintings are for ghosts. The paintings establish a comfortable destination for them to be at peace. John... we wouldn't be alive." She felt like a nurse taking care of a scared baby, soothing John's fears, letting him know what was right and what was wrong. "They are just paintings."

Frowning at her response, he pleaded, "But we would be living a dream! If we moved on together, we could live anywhere and anyway we wanted. We could be movie stars—rich, famous, attend all the big parties, do anything we wanted. Isn't that the best?" He repeated what he said to himself to ensure that he said it right to win her over to his dream.

Shaking her head in denial that he was slipping away from her, she repeated, "No, John, it won't work. I know what they're offering sounds good, but we wouldn't get what you're thinking we would get. No one's going to transform the painting into a destination set up for us. I just paint dreams. They promised me I could go home immediately without you or help them out for a while and they would let us go back to where we were before everything bad happened. No tricks, every physical thing back to the way it was. If we accept anything else, there will be a catch, something would be off, guaranteed. Do not trust any deal with them. Believe me."

Puzzled at her inability to see his dream, he pleaded again, "But how is going back to like it was better than what I'm talking about? Before, we were fighting to survive each day. If we move on, we can have everything we want. Whenever we want. What's better than that?"

Holding herself together, she pleaded with him again. "Don't fall for their promises. Somehow, something will go wrong. I just know it, you have to believe me."

Seeing how his dream and hers were further apart than ever, he said, "I don't see how it can go wrong." He stared at her a moment and continued, "While you worked for both of us to be able go back to the past, I fought for both of us to move forward to a better life. If you don't want that life, I will move on without you. Do you want to come with me or not?"

Stunned, she tried to understand how all her hard work and sacrifices were going to be for naught. With a last-ditch effort, she pleaded, "I love you, John. Don't you love me? Can't we work this out?"

"Living on my own after you got hurt, I realized what we were missing out on." He paused and looked around at what looked like their old apartment. "I don't want to go back." Knowing that she wasn't going to move forward with him into what sounded to him like his dream life, he left her.

She was alone again, but refused to cry. After what seemed like years of working to get back with John, all it took was a few moments to be over.

She hoped it was another test, not really John, but she feared that the stranger she was talking with was the real John, just not the John she loved.

She was thinking about all the work she had accomplished, all she had put up with to get John back and how he had just walked out. Almost instantly. Like her thoughts and goals didn't matter. It happened so fast, leaving her with very little time to explain much to him. Not that she knew much. She did believe she was helping out by painting for the people she met—Melvin, James, Toby, the list went on. What she had denied herself all this time, she had to face now. All the people she met were John's coworkers and probably part of the "accident". The accident that put her into a coma. The accident that John made happen.

Another person walked in. Initially, she thought it was someone else she needed to paint a picture for, even though there was no reason to paint them anymore. But as she stared at him, she began to wonder and then tentatively asked, "Sam? Is that you in a costume or something?"

"Did you know it was me or are you just guessing?" Sam asked.

She almost answered it was a guess and then decided to go with her instincts. "I can't explain it exactly, but there is a feeling of you standing in front of me, if that makes any sense."

"It does. Very few ever reach the abilities you have, being aware beyond the physical and to the essence of another. And very few succeed in winning their way back home. Would you like to return to the mortal plane now?"

Simultaneously overjoyed and dumbfounded, she said, "What? Can't you tell me what's going on first? You have to let me know if Melvin moved on? Was that really John I just saw?"

"Yes, Melvin moved on and yes, that was John. My kind can't observe everything on earth, nor do we want to, so we missed witnessing the events that led up to the accident that killed all those who died at the construction site. Afterwards, we scanned the minds of everyone near the accident, dead, alive or in between. We only found two who displayed guilt over the recent events. Someone alive – John – and someone near death – you. What we didn't understand at the time was that your feelings of guilt were over your relationship with John. It seems understanding relationships is something we could all use help with."

Not quite believing what she was hearing, she asked, "So what I have done here is sufficient atonement for killing all those people?"

"There are many factors here. For one, you didn't kill anyone. For another, a task can be accomplished in many ways and for many reasons. You see, another ability of ours is to push minds further in the direction of their predisposition. We planned on enhancing John's natural mental direction and yours before you were returned to John. That way, we would have honored our agreement with you, and yet, most likely both of you would have died or been caught shortly after your return.

"Since you were innocent, when we enhanced your natural tendencies, you became nicer. You saw the effect our pushing had on John: his belief that he was owed a better life was just starting to manifest and that was why

he set off the bomb. When we pushed him, he couldn't stop thinking about what he wanted. We weren't sure how to proceed when he died and you were still here. We thought it best if you saw him as he was." He paused and looked at her earnestly. "You had already earned your reward to return home. We are relieved that you didn't go with him."

"I guess, so am I," she replied without much enthusiasm.

"John will live a life in his picture of a Vegas penthouse. With John's nature to be never satisfied with what he has, no matter where he goes or what he has, he won't be happy. We expect he will go insane as he keeps searching for something better, something he thinks he deserves. Amazing, really. All he would have to do is stop and enjoy what he has."

"So you're saying there is an afterlife and my paintings were for more than just a resting place?"

"What happens to that which is not human flesh upon death is not something I can define in terms you would understand. Just be happy knowing your paintings will be of great comfort to those you helped along. And now it's time for your return, although we must point out the obvious in that John has passed away so we cannot return you to live with him."

"That's probably for the best, since John wasn't who I thought he was. If he stayed alive, did you think we would be happy together or did you think I would suffer after working so hard here?"

"We had trouble understanding your guilt; we certainly couldn't predict how your relationship would go. In fact, we have observed that predicting relationships is very difficult for even those who claim to be experts on the subject."

She wiped her eyes with a handkerchief she didn't even realize she had brought into existence. Sam made no comment. Not wanting to think about John for the moment, she asked, "How long have I been here? It seems forever."

"Time functions differently here. You have been here years as your kind defines time—think how long it took to guide the first spirit. When in time you will be when you return to the mortal plane, we don't know. Most likely it will be not long after the accident, although it could be years later."

She thought to herself it didn't matter how long she was gone; her old life was over. She realized how far she had drifted away from her family and friends under John's influence.

As she was contemplating, Sam continued, "When most people become unconscious, they cling to their body. Since you didn't, we had to ensure you wanted to return to yours and that answer had to come from you. That is really the test we set for you: did you want to return. You always brought John into the equation and so we tested your resolve regarding him also."

Donna thought about this and looked up to see what she thought might be a smile on Sam as he continued speaking, "We don't really feel emotions like humans, but we do have a sense of responsibility towards you for incorrectly evaluating your guilt. We also feel enlightened by observing you learn some of the tricks of this plane, the house with a couch and TV was a nice touch that few have created before. We think it only right to provide you with a rare parting gift for your un-deserved yet fruitful time here. When you return, you will remember all you've learned here about painting. Your determination to succeed showed itself as you

researched from our knowledge base of everyone who has passed through here. Your focus on painters allowed you to rapidly become a master artist. This validated to us that we are on the correct path on how we are saving knowledge before it passes away. That is your gift to us." He paused and then added, "There is one other last gift: you will remember what I look like now."

She didn't understand why remembering what Sam looked like now would matter, but she understood the implications of her ability to paint. With what she had learned, she could very well be the best living painter when she returned. She was happy with the generous gift and thanked him.

Sam acknowledged the response with a nod and then continued. "We are sorry for your lost love. But know that when we enhanced your natural tendencies, it allowed you to know your own worth. This means you have more love to give others, not worrying about yourself. We are confident you will find your true love when you return."

Giddy with excitement over her future, she started thinking about all the things she could now do and wanted to do once she returned. So many thoughts stirring around—then none.

Donna slowly gained consciousness and started to piece some of her memories together, figuring out where she was. She started to discern the sounds of medical machinery and after what seemed like a long time, her eyes slowly adjusted to see light coming in from under a door.

She shut her eyes as someone entered and turned on the lights. She heard him asking her urgent questions. She wasn't sure what he was asking as she slowly reopened her eyes to see Earth for the first time in ages. The hospital room looked glorious. She looked at the man who was asking her questions and was about to tell him to slow down when she noticed he looked exactly like Sam. "Sam?" she asked.

"No. My name is Brad. I work here." Momentarily flustered he added, "There is usually someone here who knows and cares for you and is waiting for you to wake up. I'm sorry that no one you knew was here when you finally did." He looked towards the door and added with puzzled expression, "Honestly, it is strange that I am the only person here to see this."

She thought of Sam's last gift to her and smiled as she guessed it wasn't strange at all, but rather well-placed timing. She pondered the situation and decided to ask, "Do I know you?"

Brad sheepishly smiled and said, "I don't expect you to remember me, but I had a crush on you in high school. I sat behind you in a few classes."

She inhaled deeply in a startled manner as she started to recall why the face was familiar after all. She marveled that they had been so close before and yet never connected. Neither one having the confidence to start up a conversation with the other. Thinking how school felt like ages ago and that things had changed, she asked if he was married. When he replied in the negative, she felt confident that she and Brad were going to spend a lot of time together. She got a promise from him to take her to dinner when she got out. He was smiling as he left to get a doctor to see how soon that date could be.

She relaxed in the bed, hoping it wouldn't be long until she got discharged so that she could go out with Brad and start painting again. She was contemplating how to surprise him when she eventually brought him to her first gallery showing.

Clara's Recognition

Shannon Ozog

Shannon Ozog is a writer, reader, English major and library associate — in short, a total book nerd. Favorite genres include fantasy and science fiction laced in teen drama. When she's not writing, she can be found in her native Granite Falls home baking delicious homemade pies, playing WAY too many video games and cuddling with her high school sweetheart.

A child's love for her parents is absolute — it may be tested, but it comes out fiercer and brighter in shine. But if there is anything more powerful, it must be a parent's love for their child.

Clara ran. Down the skids, down the ridges of the mountain's spine. Pebbles spilling, feet half-sliding over loose rock and moist plants. Her mother held one hand on her back to keep her steady, while her father tugged her along by the wrist. Once in a while, he'd look over his shoulder, search the sparse tree cover for their assailants, but Clara dared not look back. She heard them — even for a half-breed, she'd inherited more than enough of her father's Elven hearing. They were faint, but she heard their shouting, and their lithe feet leaping across the rock.

Mother looked about her again, dark curls splayed as she whipped her head back and forth. "We're not going to make it, Menral! They're too fast!"

Father cursed between his teeth. "I know."

The slope leveled out on another ridge and the thin forest opened once again. Stars blanketed the night sky as waning Llero was half-consumed by darkness. A foreboding sign of what was to come, or so Clara could not help but believe.

They slowed to a stop on the ridge, breathing fast and hard. Menral squeezed his daughter's hand. "How much farther?"

Clara shut her eyes and concentrated. "It's down below... I can't tell exactly where."

His gaze darted back up the mountain—bright, gentle eyes now filled with utter panic. Her mother said his name, and upon locking eyes with his wife, Menral drew the slim sword from his waist.

"Then you must go on without us, Clara," he said. "Dali and I will buy you time."

Clara stared aghast at her parents. "Wh-What? No, I can't leave you to fight them alone!"

"Your father's right, dear," Dali argued. "We would only slow you down."

"B-But..." Clara shook her head. "There are too many of them. If you try to fight, you'll die!"

"Then our deaths shall be a noble sacrifice to our goddess," said Menral, "and most importantly, our daughter."

"You can't— " she began again, but choked on her own protest as the goddess's soul swelled within her. Pulsing, hot, every hair on her body pricked like lightning strikes.

She felt like her heart might burst out of her chest, and she laid her hand over it as if to keep it in. The pain passed as before, but more slowly; she couldn't wait much longer until the goddess awakened. Whether she was ready or not.

"Clara."

She gazed again at her mother Dali, and felt her hand touch her shoulder.

"It will be all right," Dali assured her. "No matter what happens next, everything will be all right. You are our daughter. You are our savior, and we believe in you."

Tears caught in Clara's throat as Menral reached for his wife's hand, and clasped it with a nod. Human and Elf, a pairing forbidden by their laws, yet Clara had rarely seen a love in their culture as strong as the one her parents shared. The Children of the Sun were an unchanging people, steeped in tradition and discipline in every aspect of their lives, even marriage.

Yet her parents' love had changed them, helped them grow as individuals as well as lovers. Menral's hair had once been blond, but it'd darkened as he drifted further away from the Sun. And Dali, who'd once been too afraid to leave the house, strode through the city streets of Cyly with her head high and heart on her sleeve, even as the Elves tried to rip it off.

And the only thing they loved more than each other was their half Elven daughter, one of the five chosen Soulholders who would save the world.

"Go, Clara." Menral stroked the side of Clara's cheek, held it steady so she wouldn't look away. "Go and do us proud. We'll fend them off for as long as we can."

She believed them. Heart screaming, eyes begging, every fiber of her being rooted in place, but she had to believe them. She had no choice.

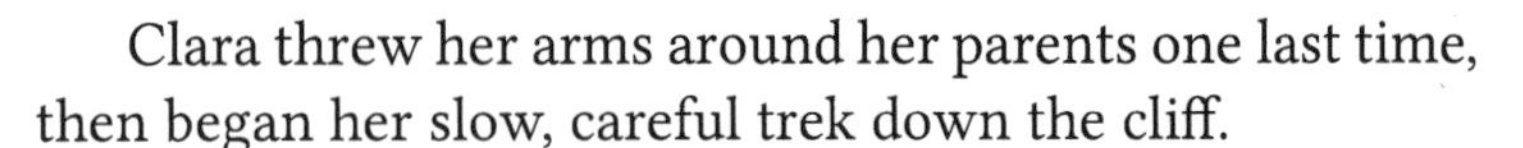

Clara threw her arms around her parents one last time, then began her slow, careful trek down the cliff.

Menral gazed after her until she disappeared from sight, one arm around Dali's shoulder. She would make it. By gods did he know Clara took after her mother, and she'd never been a quitter. Besides, she had the soul of a goddess protecting her, and he doubted the Fates would risk her death so soon.

He prayed, not for the first time, that he did not misplace his faith.

"Love," Dali whispered as she tugged his arm and turned. "They're here."

He'd already heard their approach in the crinkle of pine needles, snapping branches, and tumbling gravel kicked along their every step. But more than that, Menral sensed their intent: blazing auras, once bright with righteousness, now howling with ugly hate. All souls possessed an aura unique to them, but only a few kinds of people could detect them. Elves were one such people, gifted at empathy, but Menral need not have been an elf to know these men had come to kill them.

There were eight in all. Sun-Elves, the so-called holy children of Thgil, mortal incarnations of their chosen element. Menral found no trace of the Light God's kindness in their bright eyes, yellows and golds and silvers practically glowing against their brown skin. Unlike Menral's hair, theirs shimmered under the faint moonlight, smooth and fair and styled to complement their long ears.

One stood in the center, dressed in gilded armor. Despite all his glamor, Menral knew well that the gold served a purpose – it was one of few metals ideal for

channeling magic, especially light. His near-platinum hair was cut short, unusual for a people that longed to imitate Thgil's sacred form.

"Well well," the armored elf greeted them with open arms and a toothy smile. "If it isn't Menral and Dali."

"Danoden," Menral replied, stone-cold. "You've taken an awful many Sun-Elves into Krad's domain tonight, don't you think?"

"Taken? Oh no. These men volunteered as soon as they heard the good news."

"I don't know what you're talking about."

"Do not play this game, Menral. Did you really think we wouldn't notice you and your herd sneaking about in the dead of night?"

"That was the idea, yes."

Another laugh, but it died in moments. "Give me the girl. You do the goddess an insult to trap her within a body born of sin."

Dali took one dangerous step forward, but Menral's arm blocked her way.

"My daughter isn't here," he snapped. "Now I kindly ask you and your band to leave, or else suffer the consequences."

"Us suffer the consequences?" Danoden glanced over his shoulder, at the allies surrounding him on all sides. "I think not, old friend. We have the numbers, and you've nowhere else to go."

As much as it killed him to admit it, Menral knew he was right. His arm before Dali didn't waver, but he raised his sword at the elves with the other.

"Danoden, please," Menral urged one more time. "We were comrades once, you and I."

"Yes, that we were," Danoden sneered, and pointed at Dali. "Until you brought that bitch home and made a mutt of a daughter together."

Dali's hands flared to life with light-magic, white and gold sparks like fireworks in her fingers. With a yell, she threw a bolt of magic lightning at the elves, one that could kill any ordinary, unsuspecting spawn of darkness.

But Danoden caught the bolt in his fist. He squeezed it tight and snuffed it out as if it were a candle's flame, and his wicked smile only grew wider. "A puny effort. Your pathetic magic cannot touch the Children of Light."

"I see no Children of Light – only demons," said Dali. "You are a blight on His name. Your hatred soils it!"

"You should learn to rein in your pets, Menral," Danoden warned, and as he raised his hands, his fingers took on a vengeful gold of their own. "I can't be held responsible for what may happen to her when she bites!"

Every hair on Menral's body stood on end as magic hummed through the air. He grabbed Dali and threw them both to the ground as a crackling white beam flashed over their heads. The others linked hands and began to chant, and though Menral wasn't the most adept magic-user in Cyly, it wasn't difficult to guess their intentions.

"Fools!" he screamed. "You could bring the entire mountain down on us, and for what!? A grudge!?"

"Nay, Menral," said Danoden. "For our righteous gods, we aim to correct a mistake made long ago... Starting with your wife."

Lightning strikes sprayed from their hands and split the air in jagged cracks. Menral and Dali ducked their heads and shut their eyes, but they both knew it was only a matter of time before one of the branches found its mark. As a Sun-Elf himself, Menral was resistant to light-magic just like Danoden, but Dali was a different story. He spread

his body over hers like a shield at her back, but how long could he keep that up before Danoden and his men pried them apart?

"I'm sorry, Dali," Menral murmured into her ear. "You wouldn't be in danger if— "

"Don't say it," Dali cut him off, and craned her neck around to glare at him. "Don't you dare apologize like we've done something wrong. My loving you, the birth of our beautiful daughter—those weren't mistakes. Far from it."

Even beneath the howling wind and hissing light, he felt himself fall in love with her all over again. Dali was nothing like the Elves – unafraid and unchained to anything except her heart. His old peers had other names for those traits – wild, feral, foolish, and reckless – but it was those same traits that Menral loved most about Dali, about all Humans. Their unpredictability and their passions.

She squeezed his hand so their fingers intertwined. Two hands in dark skin, equally blessed by sunlight, bruised and battered by hardship, each filling the gaps in the other. Human and Elf, yet from his angle, no one would've seen a difference. Menral had not a doubt in his mind: this was the Elves' future. Out in the world, loving and bonding with a people other than their own. Not cooped up on a mountain top like false gods, slowly withering away as the rest of the world forgot them.

"Together, love," Dali whispered. If not for his enhanced hearing, Menral may not have even heard her beneath the crackling thunder.

He nodded and kissed her forehead. "Together."

Then they sprung to their feet. Hand-in-hand, Menral with his sword, and Dali with the blaze of light-magic.

Clara dared not look back as she skidded, stumbled, and slid down the mountain. Far behind her thunder rolled and cracked, but she couldn't turn around. If the Sun-Elves killed her parents — gods forbid — before she reached the Circle, their sacrifice would be for nothing. She would not let her parents down. She would not let her goddess down.

The pull dragged her to level ground, where trees and brush swallowed her. Hot in her chest, tugging at her heart as if it were on one end of a string. Her goddess's soul flared once again, and Clara missed a step in shock. She tumbled over rocks and twigs, covered in scratches, stones digging into her bare legs and arms — but she pushed herself to her knees and pressed on.

At last, the woods opened up. She ran faster, breathing hard, pulse pounding in her ears. Finally, an end in sight. Once the goddess woke, Clara could seek her aid and return to help her parents. She only hoped she'd make it in time.

Even in the midst of panic, once the trees cleared, Clara gasped at the Circle's beauty. Perfectly smooth, polished marble, engraved with the gigantic five-pointed star and the sacred elemental symbols. Light, Earth, Fire, Wind and Water, starting at the northern point and going right in a circle. A rainbow of gems sparkled in the night within each elemental sphere — diamonds, emeralds, rubies, sapphires, topazes, peridots... Clara had never seen so many valuable jewels, even in the Elven city.

She shut her gaping mouth and took her first steps upon the stone. Now was no time for admiring. When she reached the empty center of the Star, she clasped her hands, bowed her head, and prayed.

Help me, Clara pleaded with all her heart. *I am a Soulholder, your chosen savior and host to a goddess, but I'm helpless right now. Awaken, and make me strong!*

Light filtered through the cracks, and the spirit guardian spoke to her mind, using the old tongue. "I hear your plea, savior. Yet still you must make a choice. Will you accept the sleeping goddess within yourself? Will you pledge to give to her your life, body, and soul?"

Why must she waste time answering such a pointless question? As if she ever had a choice. As if the guardian did not already know hers.

"Yes!" Clara shrieked, and replied again in its language. "I accept, consequences be damned!"

A gust of wind blew across the Circle, tore through her hair and sent a chill through her aching bones. Clara hugged herself tight to keep her clothes from flailing about her, and had to shut her eyes to keep them from drying out.

"Then it begins!" the guardian roared. "Prepare, young Soulholder, for your awakening is at hand!"

A fire bloomed in the depths of her core, cascaded down her veins and entwined around her soul like ivy on a stone. The Guardian's voice boomed across the void, but it was dull beneath the pounding of her own heartbeat. The light on the Star changed shades from a steady white to a vibrant green and gold, and the streams etched a pattern into the blank space under Clara's feet. A flower.

The symbol of Therya. Clara recognized the carving immediately.

Indeed, my child. Who is it that speaks my name?

Clara staggered as she reached for her head. But she wasn't afraid, merely caught off-guard. Therya, goddess of nature, the woods, fertility, mother of plants and animals. Her voice filled her entire being and it still wasn't enough, shuddering in her bones and echoing off the walls of her skull. And yet, it was everything Clara always dreamed of: gentle, firm and wise. Power seeped through her every vein and held her steady like the roots and knots of a tree. And the void in her heart where the soul had slept and grasped at her with such pain, now it was full. Overflowing with warmth and completeness.

So. This was what it felt like to carry a goddess inside you.

I am Clara, she replied, in the same way Therya had spoken to her—with her focused thoughts. *It... It's an honor to finally meet you, Lady Therya.*

Therya chuckled, a ripple just beneath Clara's skin. *Same to you, my Clara. Thank you for bringing me back into this world.*

Tears sprung to Clara's eyes, and she buried her fists into them. Of the many days and nights she'd dreamt of this moment, Clara had also feared it. The Elves of Cyly were always quick to doom her, frighten her into believing the goddess would revile her mixed blood. That she would sooner destroy her from the inside out and try for better luck next cycle rather than live trapped in a body of sin. But they were wrong. Clara felt it for herself: love. A boundless love rushing into her, like the arms of a parent around a newborn child. As long as she and Therya were bound in flesh and spirit, then there was no hatred strong enough that could tear them apart.

Then she remembered. Her parents. The Cylian Elves must have caught up with them by now.

Lady Therya, Clara pleaded from within, *my mother and father, they—*

I know, the goddess answered. *They will need our help if they are to survive.* Her soul blazed, white-hot in her core and stretched all the way to her fingertips. A dizziness swept over Clara, as though besieged by a fever, but she didn't waver.

Come to me, Clara, my dear Soulholder. Come into my embrace, and let us rescue them together.

Clara didn't quite understand what Therya wanted of her. How could they embrace if they shared the same body? But once she closed her eyes, she saw her. Therya in a cloud of blooming flowers, seedlings sprouting at her feet with each step. Rich, dark skin that shined in the sunlight, and long coils of hair adorned with petals and vines. She spread her arms in welcome, a kind smile and intent emerald gaze that could melt even the sternest of men.

So she fell into her goddess's arms. Therya ran her fingers through her hair and cooed in her ear, for despite the many cruelties she'd faced on the outside, here she was safe. Protected. Loved and adored for simply being who she was. Clara—the self within her dream—closed her eyes as well, and let the goddess fill her. So long as she had Therya, everything would be all right. She would save her parents, and all would be well again.

Menral knew he couldn't allow the ring of casters to finish their chant, so he leaped past Danoden and cut down the first elf he saw. Their magic circle broken, the rest of the elves staggered in place, and he managed to wound another, a long slash across the hip.

The lightning storm fizzled away, giving Dali the time and space to cast a few spells of her own. Although her best magic would do little against the so-called creatures of Thgil, she focused all her energy on Menral, Light-blessed spells that made him stronger. She also cast a barrier around herself, a transparent, gold sphere that shimmered against the night's darkness.

With Dali's magic to empower him, Menral's blows found their mark while his enemies missed. But though Menral was a skilled swordsman in his own right, they still outnumbered him. The remaining elves recovered and drew their swords, then surrounded Menral on all sides, Danoden at the head.

Elves do not fight—they dance. A thrust, a jab. Two paces back, another three forward. Spinning and pivoting and swiftly stepping with a world of grace, always insisting on beauty even in the midst of death and violence. Another jab. A twirl. A thin slice across the cheek. It took all of Menral's concentration to block, dodge, swerve, and predict every maneuver thrown at him. He knew all of these steps, having many decades' worth of practice.

But even Elves, revered servants of the gods, make mistakes.

He'd been expecting another thrust. Instead, a pony-tailed Sun-Elf took a slash at his leg, a low sweep that sliced at his hamstrings and cut to the bone. Menral screamed as he stumbled, but before he could strike back, Danoden shoved him to the ground. He hit the dirt face-first, grit digging into his cheeks. When he tried to rise, Danoden stomped on his sword-hand and pried the weapon out of his grasp.

Danoden pointed Menral's own sword at his neck, another insult.

"You've grown soft, Menral," he sneered. "The proudest swordsman in Cyly would never have succumbed this easily."

The fallen elf spat at his feet.

"Tell us where she went," Danoden ordered yet again, "and we might grant you a swift death."

"Go to Hell."

"So you don't care at all what happens to you. Fine."

Unsure what he meant, Menral's gaze swept the ground and counted the pairs of boots encircling him. He'd already killed two, so there should be six elves left. Danoden, and four others all around him.

Danoden and four.

Menral's heart pounded between the ground and his ribs. Where was the fifth elf?

"Dali! Look out!" he shrieked, but he was too late. The other elf had snuck up behind her. He lay his palm on her magic barrier, and in a flash of gold and white, the shield dissolved to nothing. Dali began to turn when the elf stabbed his sword through her right shoulder—and kept it lodged in her, so she couldn't run away.

As the sword pierced her, Dali screamed. Tears swelling, teeth grinding against the pain, but she was still very much alive.

"So there you have it," Danoden spoke again. "One more quip out of you, and I'll have Arland here slice her to ribbons. Slowly. Painfully. As many times as he'd like."

Menral barely heard him, unable to look away from his wife. Blood was flowing out of her wound, soaking through her white gown.

"Now, I won't ask again," Danoden continued. "Where has your daughter gone?"

Dali shook her head ever so slightly, and mouthed what Menral knew she would sooner scream: "No." She would rather die than betray Clara, no matter what that death might entail. Though it tore at Menral's heart to choose between them, he was the Elf of the family. Born to a people who'd slumped into decline since the gods first descended into mortal forms, a dying race that saw fewer newborns each year. So like all Elves, he would always choose his child over anything else, savior or not. Surely, Danoden knew that as well.

But before Danoden could give the order, a flood of power washed over the elves. Though Dali couldn't feel it like they could, she followed their shifting gazes to the woods far below. Menral's breath caught when he saw the light — a gold and green beam piercing the heavens and shining like the sun, though he knew Clara couldn't house Thgil. Birds cawed and scattered from the trees as the earth trembled and sighed, for its Mother had awoken, as Menral always believed She would.

"Ahhh..." Danoden breathed deeply from the air, awestruck. "Here she comes."

She strode uphill over gravel and roots without a stumble. She still looked like Clara — wavy long hair, richly brown skin, a soft face adorned with the fine-tipped ears that betrayed her Elven ancestry — but her every manner was wrong. Chin high, arms resting at her sides, stoic and calm and so unlike the modest, shy girl Menral had raised with Dali. She stood as dignified as any queen — no, more powerful than that. Menral felt it burning off her skin, saw the air quiver with heat around her, a goddess's soul barely contained. An emerald shimmer danced across her brown eyes, coming and going like a leaf on a breeze, and Menral knew that his daughter was lost to him now.

"Mighty Therya." Danoden dared to take a swooping bow before her, even as he stood over Menral with his sword aimed at his neck. The other elves followed him, except for the one holding Dali hostage. "It is the highest honor to be within your presence."

"*Hollow words from a Sun-Elf who harms my Soulholder's family,*" said Clara, though they were not truly her words. The goddess spoke through her host, the voice of both souls spilling out in perfect unison. Menral cringed; to hear her like this was both jarring and beautiful.

"*Why do you do this, Danoden?*"

"My Lady," Danoden began again, "it is the fault of these fools here that you've been reborn into that Half-Elf's body. It was our aim to release you from imprisonment before the Recognition... But the parents were not so willing to lead us to you."

Therya's eyes narrowed. "*By release, you mean murder.*"

"Ah, murder is such a... grisly word. But a necessary one."

"*Your deluded kindness is lost on me, Sun-Elf.*" Clara's hands curled into fists as the goddess's gaze bore into Danoden, ruthless and unforgiving. "*Our forms are sacred and born the way they are for a reason. You think you know better than the Fates, mortal?*"

"The Fates have failed Elvenkind time and time again. Our kindred spirits in the seas, skies, and mountains have all but disappeared, and those who remain die a little more by season's end. I place my fate in the traditions that have sustained us for centuries, in the purity that is our Elven blood and the generations who carry it." Danoden glared again at Menral beneath his boot. "Not in a mistake bred by a traitor and his human whore."

Down on the ground, Menral squirmed. "Get out of here, Clara! You're Recognized now, just run! Run and forget about us!"

"*Do not fear, my mortal father,*" Therya spoke tenderly, all traces of her previous anger gone. "*This is what she wants.*"

Then she raised her hands high into the air, glowing with the gold and green sparks of Earth-magic. Though

Clara had never possessed such power before, any Elf like Menral could recognize an elemental sphere, from any source.

A rumble in the earth caused the elves to stumble, before its surface cracked open. Barbed vines and roots ruptured from beneath them, slithered over the dirt and up their bodies like snakes around their prey. The tangle ignored Menral, instead lashing out at Danoden above him – wrapped around his legs and arms and pulled. Panicking for the first time since he'd arrived, Danoden tried to cut away the vines with his sword, but they were too tough, and the tightness around his wrists inhibited his swings.

Dali, meanwhile, found her freedom as her captor was lost in the earthly tendrils. With a desperate cry, she pried herself free and the blade slid out of her shoulder. She tripped and fell on her knees, one hand on the ground and the other covering the bloody hole, but that did not stop her. She crawled toward her husband, blood spilling between her fingers as she inched closer. Menral reached out to her, ever conscious of the magical vine pit slinking below his arm. He crawled, too – slowly, achingly, without the help of his dead leg.

When they grasped each other's hands again, relieved smiles stretched across both their lips. Gold and white light graced Dali's fingertips as she inched closer to her husband's wound, but Menral squeezed her healthy arm and kept her still, shaking his head.

"No, Dali," he rasped, "heal yourself first."

Her face fell. "You've already lost too much blood."

"I'll be fine." Menral's smile turned grim without his meaning to. "Your blood is much more precious than mine."

Ever the stubborn one, Dali glared at him and pushed against his grip, but he wouldn't budge. So instead, sighing, she placed her glowing hands against her own wound and murmured the spell under her breath.

As Dali healed herself, Menral marveled at their goddess-given daughter and the treacherous Sun-Elves. Each of Danoden's men squirmed and kicked within Therya's vines. A desperate few tried to cast their way out, only to have their incantations silenced when the vines lashed over their mouths. And there, standing in the center of it all, was Clara, more calm and unflinching than Menral had ever seen her before. Even if she wasn't really Clara right now, there stood the girl whose diapers he'd changed, whose hair he'd brushed, whose vibrant laughter had filled his home, and whose nightmares he'd chased away with a lullaby. There stood his girl, all of his pride and joy, and She was magnificent.

"I can hardly believe it," Menral whispered. "That our Clara could be capable of such strength."

Dali followed his gaze, and once her shoulder was whole again, she nodded. "She is the Therya Soulholder now. One of five heroes who will save our world." As she spoke, she edged toward his leg; he flinched when she laid her hands on it, no matter how gently. "She learned well, from both her parents."

Proof that Elves and Humans together made beautiful children. Tears sprung to Menral's eyes, and not from the burning pain in his leg. Not at all.

With their enemies incapacitated, only one elf remained with the ability to speak: Danoden, jerking and cursing in the fit of vines and roots. Therya stepped closer to him, hands at her sides; though they no longer bathed in the gold and green light of the earth, with every step she took, magic seeped out of Therya's feet and fueled her writhing enchantment. As if the roots were an extension of herself, and she was the tree at their center.

She stopped a few steps before him, her glowing green gaze burrowing into his bones. For the first time since Menral had known him, Danoden flinched.

"P-Please!" he wailed. "My men – my men are innocent. They only followed under my orders. Do what you will with me, but let them go, please!"

As if Menral could not hate Danoden more, he had the nerve to lie through his teeth, even to mighty Therya. Judging by her narrowed eyes, the goddess didn't believe him either.

"*Those who knowingly follow a madman are as guilty as the madman himself,*" Therya snapped. "*Is this not a part of your Elven code, Danoden?*"

The other Sun-Elves began to moan. A few at a time, beneath their earthly muzzles. Danoden craned his head to see the other nests tightening, squeezing to death the men trapped inside. Bones popped, screams were muffled, and despite the rich brown of his skin, Danoden's face began to pale.

"N-No. No! We're a dying race, you cannot do this!" he cried, but nothing would change the goddess's mind now. Menral shut his eyes and bowed his head, for though they'd chased them through the woods and hunted him and his wife, he'd no wish to watch his kin die. In the dark of his eyelids, limbs broke, ribs cracked, and finally, their shrieks fell silent.

When it was over, the knots of tendrils relaxed and slithered away, depositing the bodies of Danoden's men gently on the ground.

"*You led these men to their deaths when you let your hatred blind your judgment,*" Therya continued, not a sliver of remorse in her or Clara's voice. "*You may be Elven, and you may be servant to my beloved Lord Thgil, but that doesn't give you the power to spew such hatred or rewrite fate. You and those who'd followed you tonight shall never harm another Half-Elf or her family again, nor will you ever again drag another of your kind to ruin with your folly."*

Just a fraction, the vines engulfing Danoden tightened.

"*Have you any last words, Danoden?*"

"I-I..." The elf's bright eyes glimmered in the dark, perhaps with tears. "I was wrong. O beauteous, O powerful, O Mother Therya, there is not a flaw in you or your mortal incarnation, perfect goddess. I know I don't deserve it, but I beg of you... P-Please, forgive me."

Therya eyed him a while, brown-green gaze devouring his every twitch and whimper. Until, after what felt like an eternity, the vines shuddered and slithered to the ground. Danoden fell on his knees, head low and weeping, as the magical plants withered and disappeared in a cloud of gold dust. Without another word, Therya turned her back on him and strode toward Menral and Dali.

Both parents marveled at their goddess-gift of a daughter. Dali nearly lost her concentration, as Menral felt her healing magic shudder through his leg, uncertain. But Therya simply smiled at them, as kind and gentle as any mother to her children.

"*I owe you my life, Dali, Menral,*" the goddess said. "*Had you not protected Clara when you did, I fear she wouldn't have made it in time.*"

"As was our duty, O Holy Therya," Menral assured her. "In truth, we should be the ones thanking you."

"Though we can't always be together, we will always walk beside you, Clara," Dali added, and bowed her head to her goddess, just to be clear she wasn't ignoring her. "You are our daughter, and we love you, forever and always. No matter what happens."

"Mother..." Still her voice retained the haunting echo of Therya, and yet for a moment, Clara had shone through. The tremor in her syllables, the gratefulness of her expression – those could only belong to a mortal. Flickering in and out like a dying candle, the green flecks in her eyes began to waver; soon, Clara's body would become hers again and she, Dali and Menral could finally leave the treacherous elves behind for good.

"N-No..."

But the green blazed back to life as Therya's eyes narrowed, and turned her attention back to the whimpering Danoden. The defeated elf still hadn't raised his head, but he'd begun tracing a pattern in the dirt with his fingers.

Barely visible from his angle, Menral had to squint for a better look. "Danoden? What do you want, you miserable coward?"

Danoden gave a mirthless chuckle. "You think I'll suffer... You think I intend to keep living, alone and honorless and humiliated. But my fate is not yours to decide, mutt goddess."

Still Therya said nothing, watching him intently. Menral scoffed once, but before he could scrounge together another string of curses to make even his beloved Sunlord shudder, he noticed it. The quiet, magical hum in the air, so ear-splittingly high-pitched and faint that even his Elven ears had almost missed it. That, and the glimmer of sparks at the tips of Danoden's fingers.

"I die for them," Danoden murmured, and at last, he lifted his head. Madness shone in his eyes, paired with the cold smile stretched across his lips. "And so will you."

From where he'd been tracing in the dirt, thin streams of gold and silver light poured out of Danoden's hand.

They etched and carved through the dirt until Menral recognized an Elven rune, the symbol for justice.

"*Shield your eyes!*" Therya shouted. She spun on her heel and spread her arms wide, earth-magic flaring in her palms. But before she had the chance to cast her spell, Danoden's rune erupted.

Even beneath his closed eyelids, even for one born of the Sun, the light burned. That quiet hum Menral heard before grew into a howl, scathing the ears of anyone unfortunate enough to stand too close. He dared to open one eye just a crack, and instantly regretted it: he glimpsed a cyclone of fire, white-hot and blazing, so close to Danoden it peeled away his flesh. Not even his light-blessed body could be saved.

Then a jolt wracked the earth. So strong was the eruption of light-magic, a fissure began to spread from its center. The mountain beneath Cyly had never been stable, its rocky surface prone to slides and collapses. Perfect for deterring lowly travelers unworthy of the city's walls; dangerous for anyone who wished to leave.

After falling to her knees, Therya huddled close to Menral and Dali and pressed her magic-blessed hands into the earth.

"*Come together, quickly!*"

Slabs of stone jutted out of the ground all around them, summoned by Therya. With a motion of her hands, the stone curled in over their heads and molded together until it'd encaged them in a dark sphere. Blackness swallowed them, broken only by the faint glow of Therya's green and gold magic.

Somewhere beyond the darkness of their shell, the mountain rumbled in anguish. Boulders broke apart, trees cracked and splintered. The protective sphere shuddered in place as the Elven family clung to one

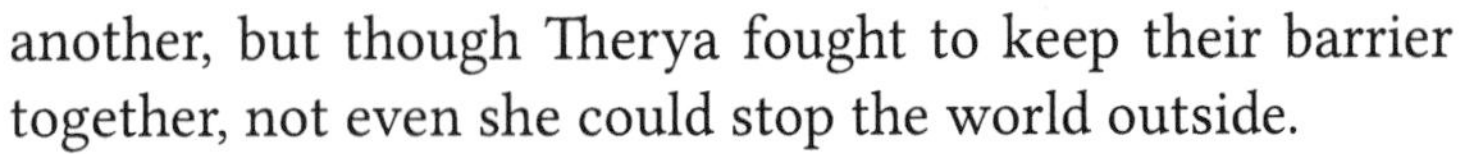

another, but though Therya fought to keep their barrier together, not even she could stop the world outside.

Next Menral knew, they were tumbling. Round and round like a pebble that'd been kicked over the edge, spiraling downward at impossible speed. Screaming with them, Menral clung to his wife and daughter for dear life, even as something heavy struck the shell and broke it open.

When he opened his eyes, for the briefest instant, Menral saw brown. Giant clouds of dust and dirt, stinging and scratching at him as he fell, down down down. He couldn't see Dali, but he still felt her fingers in his.

They were slipping.

Blinded and disoriented, Menral tried to reach out his other arm to his wife. Wind tore through his hair, his clothes, dust scratching at his skin and eyes, but he fought it all. Dali. He had to reach her, had to bring her close if they had any chance of surviving this—

She cried his name in the darkness, just before her hand slipped free of his. Menral clawed after her, but something hard hit the back of his head. The world turned black.

Pain. As her mind stirred in the depths, slowly becoming aware of her body, Clara first felt the pain. Every bone, every muscle, every sinew throbbed and ached as if covered in bruises—on the inside. The worst was her head, a dull prodding that encircled her skull like an invisible crown. She curled and uncurled her fingers a few times, just to make sure they still worked, before finally opening her eyes.

Her face lay on the ground, sideways, looking at a giant wall of broken earth. Rocks and trees of all shapes and sizes, bent and twisted and cracked. All piled on top of each other, slumped against the base of what must've been Cyly's mountain. High above, Clara could trace the path where the cliff had collapsed and skidded down the mountain side, clear of any foliage and texture that'd been there before. Dust drifted in the air, and it scraped Clara's throat whenever she breathed in.

What... She struggled to stand on shaken legs. Miraculously, despite the pain and cuts lacing her body, she wasn't badly injured. *What happened?*

Images flickered behind her eyes, blurry and dull. The Circle, beautiful and glowing, as a power ancient and warm bloomed inside her. Her father, on the ground with a sword on his neck. Her mother, bleeding out her shoulder. Elves squirming within vines. One elf in particular stood out, a man with short hair and a scowl set in his jaw. A blinding flash as the world fell sideways, and then darkness.

Warmth rushed through Clara's veins, and for the first time since her awakening, she felt Therya stir within.

I'm sorry, Clara, the goddess whispered. *I tried to save them, truly I did. But after we broke apart, I had to save you first.*

Clara's heart leaped into her throat as she surveyed, again, the tower of rubble before her.

"Mother! Father!"

Her breath quickened as she staggered toward the landslide. As she grew closer, squinting in the dark, something caught her eye. Wedged between the rocks, a tiny shape unlike the rest.

A hand.

"No!" Clara shrieked. Once she reached the spot, she dropped to her knees and dug. Pebbles spilled free as she tossed rocks aside, but she didn't care, didn't even hesitate. The deeper she got, she found dark spots on the bottoms of the rocks, stained by blood. Until, at last, she revealed an arm, a shoulder, a whole head—battered, bruised, and smashed. Almost unrecognizable, save for the dark strands of mangled hair, brown skin, and tattered white dress.

Dali's dress.

Tears poured out of her as Clara wailed, anguished, cursed the Gods and Fates a thousand times over, despite the one living inside her. They'd come so close. Mother and Father had been in her arms, smiling at her, almost freed of the Cylian Elves' tyranny. Now they were gone. Some hero she was—even blessed with the power of her goddess, she'd failed to save anyone. She, a pathetic, Half-Elven girl who was never supposed to exist in the first place.

The Elves were right. If she'd never been born, none of this would have happened. Dali and Menral would still be alive. They were dead because they'd dared to fall in love. Because they'd dared to have a child. Because they'd dared to be happy together, when they *should have* stayed far apart.

That's not true, Therya tried to soothe her. *Don't blame yourself for the evils of others. If anything... It's my fault. I shouldn't have underestimated Danoden. I shouldn't have let him live.*

"N-No..." Clara whimpered as she tried to wipe her eyes dry with her sleeve, and failed. "You... You couldn't have known. I know you wanted to protect them just as much as I did."

Clara... Therya whispered again, but didn't have the heart to continue. Still, Clara felt the emotions of her second-soul: her guilt, regret, sorrow, and anger, just as fierce and heart-wrenching as her own. At the very least, Clara knew she wasn't mourning alone. Cradling her mother's hand, Clara bowed her head and wept in silence.

Until she heard something. A muffled moan, the clatter of loose pebbles, so quiet she almost missed it. But with the help of her fine-tipped ears and the deathly silence around her, the noise cut through all her senses, even her grief.

Noise meant movement. Movement meant life.

Clara struggled to pull herself away from her mother and gazed in the direction of the sound. Pebbles and dust granules stirred in a pile of stones nearby. The boulders were humongous; Clara thought it impossible that anything could've survived beneath them. Yet, as she rose to her feet and gasped, a fist-sized rock was punched free from the pile.

From within, a hand reached through the hole and grasped at the air.

"C-Cla-ra..."

Her heart nearly stopped. "Father!"

She ran to him. Alive. Despite her earlier curses, Clara praised the same gods and Fates who'd taken away her mother. Because, by whatever miracle, they'd left her father *alive.*

She took his hand and tried to peer into the hole in the rocks, but it was too dark inside for her to see him. Trapped in such a small space, he didn't have much air left, and there was still the danger of the boulders breaking loose and crushing him. Nor did she have any idea of his condition; alive Menral may be, but in what state and for how long, Clara could only begin to guess. If she was to free her father, she needed to do it carefully.

My power, Therya offered as her warmth surged inside her. *Use it to move the rocks.*

"But I don't know how— "

I will guide you. Clara, reach inside yourself and feel me, feel the power burning bright inside you. You are my host, my precious Soulholder, and this power is yours as well as mine. You know how to wield it; trust yourself.

She didn't trust herself at all—trusting herself had cost her mother's life. But if she continued to hesitate, she'd certainly lose her father, too.

So Clara took a deep breath, closed her eyes and concentrated. In the dark of her eyelids she saw it: a gold and green strand of light, shimmering and swaying like an ocean wave before her. Unsure what else to do, Clara reached out, grasped the strand in one hand, and—*Gods!*

Warmth flooded through her from the depths of her heart. It cascaded through her veins, stretched to her fingers and toes, until she was fully aware of the Earth's every tiny breath and motion. Worms wriggling deep in the dirt, a mother deer guiding her bucks away from danger, splintered roots and branches mangled like crooked limbs... She felt it all, including Menral's labored breathing and the rocks' precarious positions around him, teetering between life and death.

She stepped back and stretched out her hands, gold-green sparks crackling in her fingers. That same glow took over the boulders, and slowly, they began to slide apart. Thanks to her goddess's guidance, Clara knew exactly which rocks to move first, where she needed to place them, and which to leave alone. But it strained her spirit, as if she were taking the stones' weight onto herself. By the time she finished, the pile had been dismantled, but a trickle of blood slid out her nose and she nearly collapsed.

Her pain was nothing next to Menral's.

"Father!" Clara gasped out as she fell on her knees and crawled to his side. Dried blood matted the back of his head and he flinched as she touched a tender spot. The rest of his body was covered in cuts and bruises, but nothing seemed broken. "I'm going to move you, hold on—"

"N-No, Clara... ahhh!"

Menral screamed as soon as she pulled. Clara checked him again for injuries – and her heart fell into her stomach. She hadn't seen it in the dark, but crushed beneath another boulder was Menral's leg. The same leg that Dali had poured her heart out to save before the mountain collapsed.

Now there were no light-gifted spellcasters nearby. Alive indeed, but Menral would never fully recover from this night. Of course, neither would she.

"F-Father, your leg..." Clara began again, but couldn't finish. He knew. Whether he felt it now or not, from the sorrowful look on his face, Menral knew the limb was lost.

He put a hand on her arm and drew her attention back. "Dali..."

Tears stung her eyes again, and she looked away. Menral choked as he too began to sob. Clara absently brushed her fingers through his hair as a means to comfort him, but she gazed only at his trapped leg, mind racing. She dared not move him or the boulder that kept him pinned; it may be the only thing that kept him from bleeding out. Necrosis would spread if she didn't cut it off, but even if she could, she had no means to treat the damage that would follow.

Am I so powerless, even still? she thought in despair. *Is there nothing I can do?*

No, came Therya's soothing voice. *Not nothing. Clara, close your eyes and listen close. Not just with your ears, but your whole body.*

She didn't understand at first. Silence consumed her on all sides, save for her father's sharp breaths and soft crying. But when she closed her eyes, she felt it. A rumble through the earth that trembled against her legs. Just as before to move the boulders, Clara put her hand against the dirt and stretched out her senses, took in all of the earth's movements.

Footsteps. Many, slow and labored, as if climbing uphill. Far behind them.

Clara gasped as she turned and peered through the darkness. Faint orbs of light flickered back at her, swaying slightly on an invisible breeze. They could be Sun-Elves, searching for Danoden and his men – or worse: for her. But with her father's life dwindling away, she couldn't afford to be cautious.

"Hey!" Clara called out as she waved her arm high in the air. "Over here! I need some help, please!"

She heard a reply, and they seemed to pick up their pace. Menral blubbered a protest, but Clara touched his cheek and held his gaze.

"Help is coming," she told him. "We're going to live, Father. Both of us, for her." And she repeated to herself silently, again and again: *I won't let you die. I am the Therya Soulholder, one of five saviors of our world, and I will not let you die.*

Lip quivering, body trembling, Menral nodded. Once she felt certain she could leave him be, Clara got to her feet and began work on his leg. Hands glowing, she moved the boulder off of him first. Menral grabbed at his thigh and bit back screams, but Clara had no time to ease him. Next, she summoned vines—smaller than the ones Therya had used in battle—and wrapped them around his leg, just above his knee. That would slow the bleeding.

She did all of this as the strangers grew closer, knowing they watched. Sneaking glances at them, Clara finally began to see them for what they were: skin tones ranging from fair to brown, humble clothes, and rounded ears. Some held lanterns that swayed on hooks, while a few others were armed, swords and spears in hand.

Humans. A scouting party, perhaps from a nearby town, sent to investigate the landslide. And, most importantly, search for survivors.

"My father is dying," Clara said once they'd crowded around her. Unsure whom to address, she met the eyes of the man closest to her, lantern light glowing soft against his reddish beard. "Please, you have to help him— "

"We will." The man spoke softly as he leaned closer, so he could see her face in the dark. "But who are you, young Half-Elf? How did you survive such destruction?"

Clara might have answered him right away if he hadn't drawn attention to her ears. Instinctively, she covered one, ran her finger against its slightly pointed tip. All her life the Sun-Elves of Cyly had spurned her mixed blood, that she was unworthy of the goddess's soul sleeping within her. While not Elven, these people were strangers to her, and they held her father's life in their hands. Just how would they react, if she told the truth?

But her mother had been human. Dali's blood ran in her veins—blood of courage, passion, and love, just as strong and steady as Menral's. If these humans were anything like her mother, Clara already knew what she needed to say.

"My name is Clara," she began again after a long hesitation. "My father and I hailed from Cyly, the Elven city above. And the only reason I'm here, still standing before you all... is because I am the Therya Soulholder."

Pockets of the party gasped and whispered to themselves, while others traced a holy gesture over their hearts. The bearded man simply stared at her a while, before he pointed to three of his men and ordered them to tend to Menral. When he gazed back at Clara again, he took a deep swooping bow.

"It is our honor to receive you, O Holy Savior," he said. "As mayor of Kortal, I welcome you and your father to stay and recover for as long as you wish."

And so Clara knew she had survived. Though not without her fair share of wounds and heartbreak, she escaped Cyly and the Elves who'd cursed her life. Forever.

Now, a greater and far more frightening path loomed ahead of her: the path of her destiny. The path that she and four others must take to release their inner gods and lift a grave curse once and for all.

The path to revive the world.

I Love You, Russian Style

Irina VanPatten

Irina VanPatten is a Pacific Northwest writer. Geography doesn't define her, though. She is an immigrant from the Republic of Moldova who arrived in America in 2002 with two small kids and five dollars in her pocket to conquer the New World. She brings the perspective of her past life experiences and combines it with modern American writing to create a unique blend of East and West in her writing.

We say those words all the time, but what do they mean and why do we say them? Do we always have a reason? Do we need one?

A loud "z-z-z" jumped out of the hot pan when I dropped the onions in. A few droplets of boiling oil splashed out, looking for John's hand to land on, but he pulled back fast. I turned to him:

"I told you not to stay so close to me when I'm cooking."

Technically, we were cooking together, but my boyfriend John knew only two dishes of American cuisine: burgers and steaks. So today's dish of salmon with a side of basmati rice and stewed vegetables was quite exotic to him. I loved having my man in the kitchen, though. There was something very sexy about John in an apron, especially since I, an ex-Soviet, was not used to the men at the oven.

"I just want to see how you cook it." John answered. "Did I cut the tomatoes right?"

"Perfect. You are quite a kitchen helper! I couldn't have cut them better myself."

"I love you!" John giggled in response.

"Did you just say that instead of thank you?"

"What do you mean?"

"Typically, when people get a compliment they just say thank you… Oh, never mind." I waved my hand, seeing a puzzle beyond comprehension on his face.

"Shit, I forgot to call…" John stepped away and dialed somebody with the one clean finger he had left.

"Mom, your doctor called and said he's rescheduling your appointment today for next week."

"I had an appointment today?" I heard John's mother's laughter on the speakerphone.

"Yes, Mom, you did. I'll pick you up next week."

"I'm glad somebody keeps track of them."

"OK, Mom. I love you," John said, ready to hang up.

"I love you too, son."

"You guys are pretty mushy with each other," I said, steering the sizzling tomatoes on the pan that gave a bright red color to the juicy mush of mixed vegetables. "I don't remember my mother telling me that even when I was a kid…"

I froze, holding the spoon in the air as if I could hear my mom's voice beside me. I don't know why the memory of this particular episode imprinted in my 6-year-old brain and never left me, even so many years later.

"What's wrong with you?" My mother yelled when I belly-flopped on the ragged country road. She yanked me by my hand and lifted me up. Then she angrily dusted the dirt off my shirt. When she saw my bleeding knee, she sighed, disappointed. It hurt, but I didn't cry. I knew that crying was counter-productive, that it would only make her mad. After my dad's early death from a devastating stomach cancer, Mom was easily irritated. But I was more concerned about my very special Mickey Mouse shirt that I was wearing, a present that my dad bought in Prague. Very few lucky Soviet Union citizens were allowed behind the Iron Curtain those days, so mom scolded him for spending all his money on presents for me and her and not buy anything for himself. Though, I didn't mind it at all. My Mickey Mouse shirt was a rare treasure in the little village we lived in and it made me an instant celebrity.

Mom brought me into the house, washed my wound and put a brilliant green antiseptic on it, that was burning mercilessly. She blew over it, then put the bandage on my knee and stroked it gently, but didn't say anything. She didn't actually have to...

"What did you say?" John asked me.

"You weren't listening to me?"

"Sorry, I got a text from Elizabeth, so I was texting her back. She is going through a break up. I think she needs her daddy for some emotional support. Even a 20-year-old needs that."

"Then call her. We're almost done. I can handle from here."

"OK," John said eagerly, as if he couldn't wait to call his daughter. He took his phone and moved to the far-right corner into the living room. While I was adding the last touch to my dish: the fresh aromatic green dill that was patiently waiting its turn on the cutting board. I have

no idea why this herb is used so rarely in America. "Dill makes everything taste better," my grandma used to say.

"How are you?" I heard John talking on the phone, then there was a long pause. He was waiting for Elizabeth to unload, I assumed.

"Aha," John mumbled a few minutes later. "Aha... What an asshole... Don't worry about it. He doesn't deserve you... Do you want me to visit you at your college? Oh, you're in the city? Then stop by... Of course, Irina will be okay with it... Then, see you later. I love you."

"Was it I love you, love you or just good bye?" I asked John while setting the table with plates and silverware. "I can't ever tell with you all."

"What do you mean?" John asked, stopping halfway to the table with the napkins in his hands.

"You see, back in the USSR," I said theatrically, spreading my arms as if I was doing a presentation on Soviet living in front of an American crowd. "Our parents and grandparents were monuments of stoicism. They were not showing their emotions easily. Even in our romantic movies, they were teaching us how not to talk about our feelings. The male characters were expressing their love with their eyes or coded words. The girls were supposed to guess when the men were in love with them, and even then, they should be proud and hard to get. So when somebody said 'I love you,' that was a life-changing event. It was not used often and only in a romantic setting. You, on the other hand, said I love you three times today but you meant three different things."

"How?"

"You said I love you to me earlier instead of Thank you. Then I love you to your mother instead of Good-bye. I think for Elizabeth was just a regular I love you, though it's still quite unusual to me when a parent says that to an adult

child, especially when you say it every time when you talk to any of your children on the phone. It's confusing."

"I never thought about it that way. But what's wrong with the parents saying I love you to their children?"

I took a pause, while setting the salmon on the plates with the white rice and topping it with steamy juicy vegetables. "I never thought about it the other way around," I said, finally sitting down and sticking my fork in the fish. "It's not wrong per se, but my question is: Why does a parent need to say it out loud?"

"Why not? Parents should always tell their kids they love them."

"Really? Always? Isn't that too much of a mushy stuff?"

John got a piece of salmon into his mouth too, but couldn't wait to chew it all before he started talking again. This subject appeared to be very important to him. "Yes, always!"

"But why? Isn't this implied? Look, I raised my kids on my own. I spent sleepless nights with them, when they were sick; I provided them with food and shelter; I made sure they had good grades, so they can go to college. Don't all of these mean I love my kids?"

"Yes, but you should still tell them you love them from time to time."

I shook my head: "John, if I tell my kids I love them, in the best case scenario, they'll be confused."

"No way!" John responded with all his certainty. "Just call your son and your daughter right now and tell them you love them. I'm sure they'll appreciate that."

"Are you serious? They have been raised differently, you know. They'll not understand this." I crossed my arms, reluctant to consider, but John insisted. I started getting curious myself: *If I go along with this, how will this turn out?*

"OK," I said, and snapped my fingers. "You asked for it." I pushed my plate aside; this task needed my full attention. John also stopped eating; he was all in, too.

First, I called my daughter Angelica, a college student at that time. She picked up the phone right away:

"Hello!"

"How are you doing? How's school?" I asked casually.

"What's going on?" she answered suspiciously. "Why are you calling?"

"What's up with this interrogation? I just called to say I love you." I squinted, waiting for her response.

There was a very long pause, then she asked, worried: "Mom, what's wrong? Are you sick? Do you have cancer?" Her grandma had died a few months ago from leukemia, so for a while she was assuming everyone had cancer.

"No, I don't have cancer."

"Did you break up with John?" She asked me with sadness in her voice. She liked John, that would have been a very sad news for her.

"No. I didn't break up with John," I answered, giving John a dirty look for getting me into this situation.

"Did Teddy Bear run away again?" Teddy Bear was the dog.

"No. Teddy Bear didn't run away." I interrupted her, "You know what, I'll talk to you later. Good-bye." I hung up the phone and looked at John.

"I told you that was a bad idea." However, I was already invested, so I dialed my son Serghei. He also picked up the phone right away. If nothing else, my kids were well-trained to pick up when their mother called.

"Y-e-e-e-s." My son answered, extending the "e" like a rubber band on a slingshot.

"How are you doing? How's school?" I started with the same questions.

"O-O-O-K."

"How are you getting along with your friends at the apartment?" I asked just to mix things up.

"Why? Did our landlord call you?"

"What did you do, that your landlord needed to call me?"

"Nothing!" He answered very fast, like a person who had something to hide. "So why are you calling?"

"I'm just calling to say I love you." There was a long pause, just like previously with my daughter, but his response was surprising:

"I love you, too," he answered. Though it sounded like a sentence with a question mark as if he was not sure how to say it. More like: "I love you, too?"

"OK, then. John and I are having dinner, so I'll talk to you later," I said, and turned to John: "You see what you did? My kids just got the shock of their lives."

John shook his head and started laughing.

"That's why you should tell your kids I love you more often, so they don't get shocked."

"Didn't you hear what just happened?" I asked, trying to piece my thoughts together for a better argument of why I was right and John was wrong but in the middle of our debate, my daughter called me back:

"Mom, Serghei just called me and he said you told him you love him, so he is worried about you."

"What's wrong with you kids?" I burst into laughter. "Can your mother just call and say I love you?"

"No," my daughter answered very firmly. "You are the Iron Lady. When I call crying, you are supposed to ask: What's the problem? And not as in 'I really want to know what the problem is,' but more like in a 'What's the big deal' kinda way. Then you are supposed to tell me to shut up and wipe my tears. If I call crying, and you tell me I love you, I would not know what to do."

"Calm down, there is nothing to worry about." I finally had to confess: "You see, I'm learning this new thing that John teaches me to say I love to my kids. Apparently, it's good for parents to do that."

"Just go back to normal, Mom," Angelica said, with relief but with annoyance in her voice. "You almost gave us both a heart attack."

"So did our experiment fail?" John asked me when I hung up.

"It all depends. Maybe it's time for me to smooth out my sharp edges. There is no need to walk around like a smile-less KGB agent all the time, now that I left my old country behind... Well, let's clean up the dishes." I got up with my dish from the table. John took the dish from my hand:

"Let me do it. You cook the dinner. I'll do the dishes."

"I love you," I said and smiled mischievously.

"Is that a 'Thank you' or a 'Love you,' Love you?" John smiled back.

"Come on, don't get used to it!"

Medium Orange

Mary Salamon

Mary Salamon resides in the Pacific Northwest and is the founder of the Creative Writers Group in Everett WA. She was the publisher of Marysville Tulalip Life Magazine. She writes fiction, non-fiction and articles for the local community. She is a mother of three sons and has five beautiful grand-children.

Some things happen for a reason. Especially for those among us who know their purpose in life, it is important not to give up hope–it might sour your sweetness!

There once was a beautiful, round medium orange. It shared space with other oranges in a bag at the grocery store. One sunny afternoon, a lady named Jane walked by the bag of oranges and placed them in her cart to buy. The medium orange became hopeful, knowing that its purpose would soon be fulfilled. Lady Jane took the bag of oranges home, along with the rest of her groceries.

The Medium Orange watched Lady Jane with anticipation, wondering when she'd take him out to be eaten. Day after day, Medium Orange kept watching and waiting, as Lady Jane came into the kitchen and made lunches for all her children. She would place a sandwich, chips, and a cookie, and then grab an orange from the bag where Medium Orange stayed. She would grab the orange on the left of Medium Orange and the orange on the right of Medium Orange; she even grabbed an orange behind Medium Orange.

Medium Orange began to wonder if his destiny would ever be fulfilled: to give nourishment and sustenance to the person that would peel his hard shell and consume his little arms one by one. Medium Orange heard the lady Jane say that oranges provided vitamin C, which is really good for small children's bones and teeth. Medium Orange waited patiently, hoping that he would be picked before his skin turned green.

Then one day, the lady Jane came in and started to make her children's lunches. She made the sandwiches, grabbed the chips and cookies and then turned to the bag of oranges and took Medium Orange out and put him in the lunch box. Medium Orange was not only thrilled but excited and relieved; finally, his destiny would be fulfilled. The little lunch belonged to Lady Jane's son named Nick.

At lunchtime, Nick grabbed his lunch box and headed outside to sit with his friends at the tables. Nick ate most of his sandwich, half of his chips and finished off his cookie. Medium Orange waited to see when Nick when would take him out and start peeling his hard skin, and eating his juicy arms, but all of a sudden, he said, "I'm full, who wants my orange?"

Medium Orange couldn't believe what he'd just heard. Nick didn't want to eat him. All the boys that Nick was sitting by said they didn't want Medium Orange either. Then Nick blurted out, "Okay then, I'll just dump it in the trash."

Medium Orange quaked with fear, "No, no, Nick can't dump me in the trash—I have to be tasted, I have to be eaten, I have to be enjoyed by someone, or I have been grown for nothing." Just as Nick was about to toss Medium Orange in the trash can, a little girl named Susie cried out and said, "Wait, I'll take your orange and give to my little sister at home. She loves oranges."

"Okay," said Nick and tossed Susie the orange.

Medium Orange was so relieved that he wasn't going to the trash can.

After school that day, Susie's mother was waiting in the car to take her home. She jumped in the car with Medium Orange safe in her lunchbox.

That night, when Susie's mother was cleaning out Susie's lunchbox, she noticed Medium Orange in the box and asked Susie about it.

"Susie, where did you get this orange?"

"Nick, a boy in my class, was going to throw it in the trash, I thought Kimmi would like it."

"Yes, she would," said Susie's mom and took Medium Orange out of the box and placed him on the kitchen counter to give to Kimmi later on to eat.

Later came, then much later came, and then the lights in the kitchen went dark, leaving Medium Orange all by himself on the kitchen counter.

"What happened?" he wondered. Didn't Kimmi like oranges?

Medium Orange became very sad and almost started to cry. "Why doesn't anyone want to eat oranges?" he wailed.

After a very long time, the kitchen light came back on and a man walked in. He grabbed a tall cup from the cupboard and poured a dark liquid into it. He glanced over at Medium Orange and said, "Perfect, I can have you for a snack at work."

Medium Orange thought he was supposed to be for Susie's sister Kimmi, but this man needed to eat, too, so Medium Orange was more than happy to be consumed by him. The man took Medium Orange to work and placed him on his desk. Later that morning, the man's boss came to his office and said, "Bob we need you in the conference room for a meeting." Bob left his desk and forgot about Medium Orange.

Medium Orange sat at the desk and waited and waited. The whole room went dark again, and Medium Orange became filled with sadness and started to cry. "I will be turning green soon, and no one is ever going to eat me."

All of a sudden, the lights went on in the room. Four people came into the room, two women and two men. They were pushing carts and going from desk to desk taking out the trash cans and emptying them.

One of the women came to the desk where Medium Orange was and emptied the trash basket, then to Medium Orange's surprise, she picked up Medium Orange and said, "I'm going to take you home to my daughter Lucinda," and placed Medium Orange in her pocket.

Hours later, the woman came home and took Medium Orange out of her pocket. She started calling out "Lucinda, Lucinda, honey I'm home." Lucinda's mother walked up some stairs and went into another room. It was Lucinda's bedroom. Lucinda was sitting up in the bed playing with her dolls. There was a box of tissues, cough drop medicine, and a jar of Vicks vapor rub on a little table next to her bed. "How are you, Lucinda?" asked her mother.

"Not good, Mommy, I hate this cold and cough."

"I know, honey; colds are no fun. But look: I brought you this nice sweet, juicy orange. It tastes good and is very good for you, especially when you have a cold."

"Thank you, Mommy," said Lucinda as she took Medium Orange in her hands.

Medium Orange was so happy, not only would he finally be eaten, but he would be eaten by a little girl who needed him more than all the others. Lucinda began to peel away at Medium Orange's hard shell. Little sprays of joy came out of Medium Orange, and he smiled as Lucinda began eating his first arm.

Sex in the Bay of Cats

Polypsyches

Gregory Roberts-Gassler, a.k.a. Polypsyches, is a screenwriter, playwright and novelist in no particular order, and moved to the PNW shortly after getting his MFA in Dramatic Writing. His stage adaptation of Pride and Prejudice was performed a while back in Asheville, NC and his novel Calliope, My Muse is available on Kindle and will be for the foreseeable future.

Meeting someone at a bar can be fun, but sometimes there are consequences. We think we know what those consequences will be, but what if things were different?

This is how things happen in the Bay of Cats.

A woman is out one night with her friends. They all have a well-deserved night off and they're enjoying themselves. All day, these wealthy women have been at home running their households. They've been meeting with business partners, and in what little spare time they've had left, they've been contributing to the education of their heirs – or arranging to make new ones. All deep, demanding work, with very little time for socializing with their peers. They need this, if only to remind themselves that they are none of them alone in this toil. If only to have some actual adult conversations.

The bar they've selected for their revels is a slightly shady business near to the barracks. Scandalously close to the soldiers. But when they come inside, there are only a few men quietly keeping their eyes averted, not wanting to draw attention to themselves, and one woman already at the bar, desperately trying to buy a drink for the most attractive of them.

The waiter, a spry sylph of a man with a shining, smiling face and a tight little bottom, shows the group to the best table near the bar and lets them flirt with him and fawn all over him. It is his job, after all, to keep the women happy.

"I'd like nothing better," says one of the friends when he leaves, "than to see just how long that strapping young lad could handle me."

"As if you could handle him!" says another.

"Is that the kind of father you'd want offspring with?" asks a third, prompting some awkward looks. This one has had only sons so far and fears now that if others rely on men from lower classes, she might never make suitable alliances. It has been on her mind.

A fourth friend finally cuts through the tension and suggests, "Who said anything about children? He'd still be a heck of a ride!" to which the women toast.

All but one, that is. There is one woman among them who does not share the others' tastes. This pretty young thing taking their orders is fine for looking, but too lanky and bony for other uses. That's not how she likes them at all.

"Well, then how *do* you like them?" asks one of her friends, and as if on cue, in steps a soldier.

The soldier is not there alone. He and his friends have come from the barracks. It is the first night off they have had in quite some time, and their conduct must be very good indeed for them to have earned it, but they have been to this establishment before. They know that it is usually not all that crowded, and that they are not as likely to be cold-shouldered out.

Still, they are only ever tolerated with folded arms rather than welcomed. Their money is good, but when the waiter approaches them, they can tell that his smile is forced. He is here for the women. They are the ones with money to spare and spend and the soldiers can see now that this was the wrong night to come here. The women are all comfortably dressed, like mothers. Mothers who own land. Mothers who own farms.

The waiter puts them at the table at the front, by the exit. This will make things easier on all of them if and when they are kicked out for riling up. They try to indicate to the waiter and to the tender behind the bar that they won't make trouble, but the unease is palpable. As if they'd ever do such a thing, as if they'd ever carry the violence that poisons their lives into this sanctuary. But how can this twig of a man know what that means to them? A short, skinny grunt of a thing—aye, but a short, skinny grunt who has a decent kind of job. No doubt fancies himself a "real" man. An honest man. One who can make a living helping people, serving food and drink for nourishment, rather than being relegated to more odious tasks.

Like killing people.

Trouble finds them, though. The biggest of the soldiers happens to glance in the direction of the women at their table in the back. He doesn't want to. He knows that he shouldn't, but he's drawn, and he catches her looking. One of the women, she has her eyes on him.

She likes the look of him. She could spot him even out of uniform from that chiseled physique. It's those arms: how the veins show, as if he'd only just come from building houses, from lifting large boulders after a rock slide or tossing tree trunks into a river to stem the tide of a flood. The sorts of things men do. The heavy lifting they're built for.

But this isn't just a man and lifting boulders is not what he's for. This is a soldier. When his food comes, she watches how he holds his knife. There is no elegance to it, she finds, only a utilitarian brutality. She really shouldn't look at a soldier, she reminds herself. It's a secret burden. Almost shameful, that she'd even want to. But there's something about that raw power that makes her want to wrap her lips around his jugular and drink deep.

He can feel her eyes on him, stroking him silkily where his shoulder meets his neck, trying to make him look back at her.

But what will happen if he does? "We shouldn't be here," he tells his comrades.

"It would be rude to just leave," they point out.

But soon enough, it's the women who get up and gather their things. A few of them are uncomfortable being around soldiers. "The sorts of things they do!" They know such things are necessary, but who ever wants to be reminded of them? "What would people say?" As they pass by the soldiers at the door, most of them either avert their eyes or glare at the men, but the last one out runs her finger along the shoulder blade of the big one, closest to the door, and makes him cringe. She reminds him that sometimes, the one thing more dangerous to him than a woman who's afraid of men, is a woman who isn't.

"It isn't our fault," the soldiers like to reassure themselves. "We didn't choose this, but now that we're here... Well, someone has to do it."

They can all pretend he was talking about the soldiers' life, but everyone noticed what happened with that last woman. They can't talk about it. The woman is gone, but they feel certain they will see her again before the night is out. They can't risk accusing or implicating her, but they all send good thoughts to their comrade, as though to reassure him "It's not that bad. It's not like she'll try to keep you. She only wants you for one thing and then it's back to the barracks. Might as well lie back and try to enjoy it."

It isn't the act itself that scares him, though.

The evening runs down pretty quickly after that and the soldiers leave the waiter to his fuming. Outside, they pretend they do not see her in the nearby shadows. "Well, I guess that's it for us," say his companions. "See you in the morning?" She watches them leave. Are they throwing him to her, glad each that they're not the victim this time 'round, *Or is he sloughing them off?* she wonders. Have they been egging him on, nagging him not to go through with it? *Men are so deliciously inscrutable...*

But that isn't it, quite. It's just the safest move for them, really. For all of them. If they acknowledge her first before leaving the one she wants, it makes the encounter public, which could embarrass her. If they acknowledge her and bring him along, in defiance of her, they are at her mercy. She is a woman—a lady of a certain class, even—and what are they but the scum-hunting scum who serve at her beck and call? What can they do? The unthinkable? Even if they wanted to, even if they could get away without being caught, blame would find its way back to the barracks. And besides, what's the harm in her fun? There are none to be hurt by women's urges.

There are dangers if he goes with her. But far fewer than in courting her wrath. What could she be thinking, out here in the night, as she stalks him? Does she imagine him to be innocent to the ways of women? Hapless prey? Is she fond of the chase? Or does she imagine he wants it every bit as much as she wants him?

Perhaps she doesn't think any of those things. Perhaps she only thinks of herself.

"Hey," she tells him. It's all she says with her tongue, but her eyes, her shoulders and her hips say more, out here in the darkness.

"Hey." His tone is illegible. It makes her dizzy with mystery—these inscrutable men! Who ever knows what they're thinking? Is it of the mead she's just watched him savor with such rapt attention? Is it of the things she will do to him soon, and he to her? Or are his thoughts darker still? The kinds of battlefield vistas and tableaus he'd never dare speak of here, lest the moon should whisper.

"Are you done for the night?" she asks. It's a risky open. Maybe she's wanting to give him a chance—even if he has been abandoned and has little choice now. Illusion is everything.

"Yes," he says. Again, it's all that he says. Simple, to the point.

"You got someplace to go?" By now, she's sidling up to him. Bolder.

"I do," he says.

She stands just under him, close enough to breathe the same air. She looks briefly down his lips to his chest before finding his eyes again. "Is that where you want to be?" And then she holds his gaze.

He takes a breath so deep his nostrils flare, which puts a curl to her lips. "No, ma'am," says the soldier.

Well, then, thinks the lady, *I guess you're mine for the night!*

Their talk is small on the way to the lighthouse. Nothing real or pertinent. Conjecture on the sky, on the meaning of clouds in the starlight, the patterns of waves in the bay. She talks about patterns and waves and the nature of the universe because she has had the benefits of an education. Philosophy and science were her favorite subjects in school, and she enjoys having a captive audience on whom to impart her garnered wisdom, even if he is only a man.

Men are not fit for such abstract musings. They don't have the build to sit down and read—it's too hard on their backs. But that's not why he has trouble paying attention to her. It isn't that he can't follow, he just has other things on his mind.

Instead, he worries about consequences. Not just the obvious consequences to him if they are discovered, but the long-term, as well. What if she becomes pregnant? Would she tell anyone? Is there any chance she might want him around? Absurd. Ludicrous. Any child she bore hence would be a part of him he could never recover, something lost, like a limb or a piece of his chest.

And besides, would he even want that? Is he capable of coming back to this real life after where he's been? Either way, he knows he'll never hear from her again after this night. This night will be a scar. So why does he go with her?

He's only a man. He doesn't have any answers.

Lighthouses are used as romantic abodes all across the Bay of Cats. They don't even pretend. At least six rooms are maintained in every one by the lighthouse attendants, contributions expected from the ladies upon receipt of the key. This one has two rooms open and she takes the one at the top and pulls him along behind her by the eyes.

Don't think about it, he tells himself when she opens the door. Times like these are for feeling, not thinking. But what he feels is a nauseous mix of anticipation and angst, and his head is swimming. Right up until he closes the door and she is upon him.

First, it's her hands on his chest. The dark meat of his pectorals have a static energy in her palms. She looks up at him, his eyes so far above hers. Then she leans forward and rests her forehead on his chin.

Is this really the first time our bodies have touched? she wonders.

He thinks it odd.

"I've never been with a man as tall as you," she confesses. "I've always wanted to stand under a man like this and..." She pushes her forehead into his chin and he can't think why. It's not unappealing, but there's an aggression to it.

She feels like she's been holding tension there, in her forehead, and it's finally ebbing away. She moves her head to the side, sliding different parts of her face over his like she's using his chin to massage herself. He doesn't quite understand what's going on or why, but how can he refuse her? What would happen to him? Finally, she bends him down towards her. Their eyes meet and for a moment their lips rest on one another.

The soldier does not disappoint. Soon, she has lost herself in the sheer mass of his sinews. The hulk of his flesh more than covers her body and blocks out the light

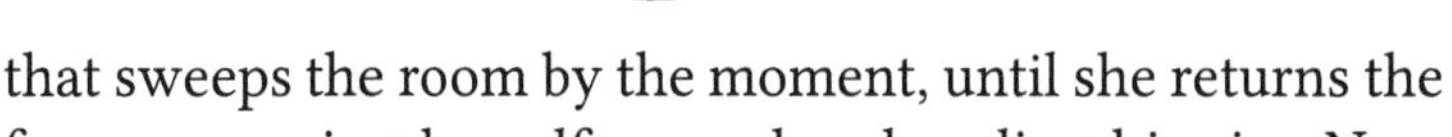

that sweeps the room by the moment, until she returns the favor, wrapping herself around and sealing him in. Now she has him in her grasp and there is no more escape.

She feels like a queen. Like a hostess welcoming a foreign ambassador into her most secret council chambers. Oh, the deals they could make! But to him, she is the predator who has already caught him, the snake wrapping around his torso to squeeze the life out of him, the better to digest the parts of him she wants most.

He feels like an animal, driven by primal need, but not the right one. He knows his future could hang in the balance, so he is fighting for his life, a rabbit in the thicket waiting out the wolf, a fly on a web hoping the spider will be quick enough about it.

"What's it like?" she asks him afterwards. They are intertwined. Her arm is across his chest, drawing her nearer into it; his arm is under her neck, supporting her head like a newborn, making her feel safe. His other arm, though, is at his side, stiff, hand in a fist. The last thing he wants to do is talk.

"What?" he breathes, reluctant to betray that he's awake.

She presses her fingernails over his heart. "Killing people."

His breath catches. She is not supposed to ask those things. She is not allowed to. But who is going to stop her? Who would believe that she had if he told?

Death is not a taboo subject, of course, in the Bay of Cats. Not as such. How could it be? People die all the time from illness or accident or disaster. They are talked about; how they happened, how to prevent them, how the events are to be recorded and remembered. There are natural causes to be served, but killing? Even killing in the name of their continued safety...

"Have you?" She seems intrigued now. He has not told her he hasn't. He has not said anything, but of course he is a soldier and the question is there, between them. "Have you?" There is something more to the question, something darker, deeper inside. The dessert at the end of a satisfying meal. She enjoys this question—he can feel her heartbeat through his ribs, slow but harder in anticipation. She will enjoy the answer even more.

He closes his eyes. "Yes."

She skips a beat. "Who was it? Was there more than one?"

"I am a soldier," he reminds her.

"I know. I know."

"Why do you ask such a thing?"

She shifts, shrugs. He wonders if she is even capable of that kind of self-reflection. "I've just always... wondered..." Stories about soldiers, about warfare or about violence of any kind, are scarce in the Bay of Cats. It's considered indecent. Consequently, there is widespread misinformation about the nature of violence and the final result is this perverted sense of curiosity. She traces tiny spirals on his skin with her nails, brushing up the occasional chest-hair. "Why won't you tell me?"

"Because it's a terrible thing," he says. "A thing no one should have to know."

She pushes herself up level to him to look in his eyes. "But don't you feel pride?"

Now it's his heart that skips. "Pride?"

"For the work you do. Doesn't it— "

"No."

She studies his face. "Why not? You keep us safe. They're barbarians— "

"They are people."

"It's not like they're innocent."

The question he wants to ask in return is not one that can be uttered aloud. It rests in the eyes of the barrack-dwellers when they find each other at night, and it waits for him in mirrors. *Are we?* But it is not a question that she needs protection from. He does not withhold it for fear it would shatter her mind – the minds of women are made of sterner stuff. He doesn't ask the question because the question is dangerous. For him.

In other parts of the world, men are in charge. They have the power and the women are silenced. Not just silenced, though. He knows the kinds of things that happen in other lands because he has seen the effects firsthand. All the soldiers have – the only people not sheltered from such evil. And yet there is a bitterness, there. There has always been some resentment in the ranks. *Why do they get to make all the decisions?* all too quickly turns into *Why can't we be more like them?*

"Is it true what they do to people?" she asks.

"Some of it."

"Is it true that they..." She struggles to find a word. A word that doesn't exist in the Language of Cats. It's a word that doesn't exist because there isn't a need for it. It simply doesn't happen. So she uses the Kardoli word. "That they do that to women?"

He knows that they do. He recalls one day his regiment came upon a village too late. He happened upon a house they had burned. The girl there, she was barely adolescent and curled into a ball in the corner. She wouldn't let him touch her, and that's how he knew.

"Why would they do that?"

"It's the way they are trained," he tells her. "The men are told to do it. They think that... They think it will make women subservient."

"To them?"

"To men."

"But that doesn't make any sense."

"And since when has that stopped anyone?"

Finally, she rests her head on his chest again. He prays for sleep, but she just will not let him. "I don't think that would stop me," she says.

He cannot say that he disagrees, but "You shouldn't talk about things that you don't have experience of."

"How would you know what I've had experience of?"

He has no answer for that, but he remains doubtful.

"I had a man approach me once. A foreigner, from the Starlands. He had that look in his eye. You know?"

He assumes it was the look she had had in her own earlier this evening.

"I knew—I just knew he wasn't going to take no for an answer."

"And did he?" He doesn't want to ask the question, but she needs him to.

Once again, she grips him tight. "I didn't give him the chance." She draws her head up, whispers in his ear. "I drew him in and had him throw me up against the wall like an Amazon. I thought he might kill me." Lightly, she puts her lips to the lobe of his ear. "It was the best I'd ever had. Till tonight."

His breathing is ragged. Half of it is rage, but he can feel her gearing up for more and hates himself for following that lead. Trying to revive a topic that's dead to her now, on a subject she is too sheltered to understand and that he hopes she never will, he insists, "It's not the same."

She coils her fingers through his hair and tugs. "Then show me."

The next morning, the woman awakens feeling better than she has in years. More fulfilled. She has the covers all around her, but soon realizes that there is no boy... She thinks he has left already, but she turns. He is turned away from her, curled up on his side, naked and in foetal position.

She assumes he's asleep, but he's not. He has been awake for quite some time, but didn't want to move, lest he disturb her. He didn't want to wake her up and risk a conversation. If she wanted to talk, let her be the one to do the waking.

But she doesn't want to talk. Instead, she leans down and plants a single kiss on his broad, bulging shoulder, then pulls the covers over him and tucks him in, which makes him feel guilty, of course. He shifts, changing his mind, indicating he might be waking up, but then he hears the door open and close. And then he feels relief, and then he feels guilty again that he feels relief. And in spite of himself, he feels sorrow that the door has closed.

It takes her most of the walk home to come back to herself, to remember she lives in a real world with rules and propriety, not one where respectable women go around reaping seeds from soldiers in late-night light-house trysts. That was some other world, some fairy realm. But it takes strolling through the early morning mists to remind her.

At home, she finds her children in their grandmother's care. "What are you doing here?" she asks her mother. "Don't you have a council meeting?"

"You mustn't begrudge an old woman her grandchildren," her mother persuades her.

But that isn't the problem here. She told her brother to look after them. "He spends all day in the fields with his friends just harvesting corn and then thinks he can get out of helping to raise his niece and his nephews? Well, come on then—where is he?"

"Oh, he muttered something about a friend down in the Copper District."

"The Copper District!" Oh, she knows exactly what "friend" he's "visiting", and after a brief leave-taking with her own esteemed mother, she storms off there to scold him.

Her brother did genuinely think he was being discreet running around with that tramp. She finds them exactly where her spies said they often met: in the shed behind the slum development where the girl lives. Little houses like this are often used by low-class women for privacy, to keep their brothers and sons and uncles from the burden of the details of their illicit affairs. Men know not to go there uninvited—but other women?

She practically knocks down the door. "What are you doing?" her brother demands when she charges him and grabs him by the ear.

"You think you're so smart, do you? Think you can keep it a secret?"

"You can't keep me away from her!" her brother insists. "I love her!"

At this, his sister laughs. "Oh, to hear a man talk about love! As if you were capable of it! And did she say the same? That she loves you?" She turns to the woman he's

been lying on, now she's closed her legs and stood back up. "I know her type," says the righteous sister. "Look at her! Poor. Entirely without class. Oh, I know her, all right. The kind who'll trap your seed. And then what good will you be?"

"It's not like he'll run out," the woman protests.

"We need him for trade!" She lectures the woman like she's an imbecile. "He's good stock! Desirable! He can get good children on our trade partners!" She turns back to him. "But if they find out you've had some bastard" (though the word isn't quite used the same over there) "with a ratty wench— "

"She's a university teacher!" the brother protests.

"Does she have family?" asks the sister. Rhetorically. "Does she have land?"

"She has family," the Professor interrupts her. "She just wasn't as fortunate to be born into a family with wealth. All I have is my education and I've had to work for that!"

"It isn't fair," says the brother. "It isn't fair I can't seek out love! It isn't fair that you throw me to the whirlpools and the fly-traps and don't let me out otherwise, while you can just skitter around munching up anything that looks right— "

She strikes him in the face.

"I am your sister," she says, "and you will respect me and do as I say."

"Because I'm just your property, is that it?"

These are not her brother's words, though—not as she knows them. So she rounds on the lover. "This is your doing, isn't it! Stuffing these lies in his head, this nonsense!"

"What's nonsense," says the Professor, "is that we've spent the last five thousand years locking up the potential of half our population. How many brilliant scientists, engineers or artists have we lost out on just because we weren't willing to let them learn?"

"They had other uses!"

"So did we," the Professor returns.

"Enough!" As a woman of some nobility, she feels the need to command the room, as it is clearly getting out of hand. "You have no rights to him," she says to the Professor. "You have seduced him away from his family obligations and taken advantage of his innocence." (or perhaps ignorance, as they are the same word in the Language of Cats) "And you will never have a child by him."

"I will never have a child by anyone," the Professor confesses. "I'm barren."

This comes with an itching of guilt, but not of surprise. "All the more reason," says the righteous sister, "not to waste his seed on the likes of you."

"Of course," says the Professor. "Because sex should only ever be for procreation and never for pleasure – is that it? Or love?"

But love is the last thing she has on her mind right now, after the encounter she had last night. The last thing she *wants* to think of.

The soldier doesn't leave their lighthouse room for quite some time after she does. He dreads the return to reality far more than she, not just because he hates the soldiering life, but because he knows there could be consequences. And probably will be.

At the barracks, his friends from last night catch up with him. They don't ask him how it went. They could be overheard, but more importantly, it isn't the kind of thing soldiers should talk about. There are acts of creation

and then there's the stuff that soldiers do. Mixing the two would be dangerous—think what that could bring into the world! Yet another reason for him to feel guilty about his encounter.

"It's a good thing you're back," says one. "The sergeant was asking about you."

"He was worried," says another. "We wouldn't want the Captain finding out, would we?"

But in the mess-hall at meal-time, there is a tension in the air that surrounds him. He can see one of the other men looking at him, a smaller man. A man who looks more respectable, lean and spare and less like a barbarian chieftain.

"You weren't in your bunk last night," says the smaller, less threatening man. He has a look of concern on his face. "Where were you?"

"We had the night off," says one of his companions.

"Oh, yeah? You guys got back all right."

"Just drop it, OK?" He has to admire his friends for sticking up for him.

But the small man is playing a game. "No, no, no," says the concerned fellow-citizen. "This is all of our business, too. Were you out uh..." He lowers his voice. "Doing something you weren't supposed to?"

The rules of this game are simple. The rules are, no string of words is worth coming to blows over. A reputation can be harmed by words, for sure, but not as much as harming someone's face.

So he tries to ignore his accuser.

"I wanna know," says the smaller man, "what kind of shenanigans you were up to. Huh?"

The larger man tries to focus on his food.

"Did you find a girl? Huh?"

The larger man grips tightly the knife in his hand.

"Did she take you back to her place? Nah, no one'd be seen with you even at a lighthouse."

That was too close to home. Too close, and people are starting to listen in.

"You probably had to take her on the street. Is that it? Is that what happened?"

Leave it alone.

"Is that why you smell so bad?"

It's only your reputation. Only ego. Don't let it—

"Lady Love, I bet it is! Who'd ever sleep with you? Mother Nature!" The smaller man shakes his head. "I'll tell you what, I sure hope you didn't take her against her will, did you? Did you? Oh, I bet you did! And I bet you let your buddies watch, too!"

And that's it. If it were only for his own sake (that's what he tells himself), but now he's implicated his companions in his guilt. It is not for men to govern the behavior of others, but this? It is for men to prevent the incursion of barbarity. *He must be silenced!* They aren't words, but some sort of primal imperative...

"It took four men to pull you off of him," the Captain informs him during their face-to-face. "That poor boy was about a third your size—what in the world possessed you to attack him?"

She is exaggerating. It was a single blow that didn't even break his nose, but even so, it was still too much. "He impugned my honor," he says through gritted teeth. "And the honor of my men."

"Your honor?" At this, she closes his file and folds her hands across the table. "Is your honor such a great, important thing that you think it worth killing a man for?"

He knows he has done wrong, knows he lost that game, so he does not answer.

"You know how important it is," she continues. "Men like you..." She runs her eyes up and down his torso. "You should never respond to the aggression of smaller creatures, even when it rises to meet you."

"Yes, Captain."

"So why did you?" She leans back again in her chair. "Tell me more about this honor you protect."

He was not expecting quite this sort of tribunal, so it takes him a moment to formulate it. "I have always been... large. Imposing. People have always been afraid of me. Just from looking at me. I work very hard, and always have, to keep innocent people from feeling like they need to be afraid of me. It has always been a burden and a barrier. So when someone like him challenges the truth of my kindness..." He catches himself. Never refer to any kindness of your own. You are not kind. You are a man. It is for others to call you kind, and for you to give them a reason. "I was wrong. I allowed my emotions to get the better of me and I disproved my own point. I admit that. But by bringing my men into it, he cast doubt on them, too, when it was my guilt—and that, I couldn't allow."

"What was it that he said?" asks the officer, her eyes nowhere but on him.

He doesn't respond. He swallows.

She leans forward. "Where did you sleep last night?"

And that is when he understands. She knows.

Now the commander stands up and he stays silent before her. She comes around the desk, stepping slowly, as if to show off her legs, and sits on the arm of his chair. He makes room for her as she reaches across him, pressing him down into the lining. Then she whispers in his ear, "And how do you think all that is supposed to make me feel?"

She's uncomfortably close to him. Not as uncomfortably close as they've been before, but he can taste her breath in his mouth. And what can he do? That's the problem with being a large man: the whole world is at your mercy, which puts you at the mercy of their scrutiny.

"What did you do to her?" asks the Captain. "That poor, poor woman?"

"Please," says the soldier.

"Yes," says the officer. "Yes, I shall do as I please."

He knows that she will.

And as she does so, she asks: "Who was she? Tell me her name!"

"Why?" asks the soldier.

"I need to know," says she, "I need to know who else has had you!"

There is something ridiculous, not just in her tone but the very nature of the command. Something possessive.

Something threatening.

"You'll know well enough," he whispers at her, "when her time comes!"

There is a moment in between where she stops and pauses and decides that yes, "her time," that's really what he said.

She disengages. She calls him a name that does not translate well as "bastard" or any other common word used elsewhere for upstart males. In the Language of Cats, she calls him brutal and heartless and sexually unadventurous. "How dare you?" she demands. "How dare you bring that up?"

But he knows that she's wanted a child. He knows what it means to her that she can't. So he doesn't back down, doesn't apologize. She has taken every other weapon from him. Now, he has only words and silence.

"Well, then," she says, straightening out and taking her seat again, as though she hadn't just had him. "You admit it, then? Your guilt?"

Still, he doesn't speak. He doesn't have to. Nothing more will work, even if he wanted to prevent it. It is to be the worst for him, just as he had feared. There are silver linings, to be sure, but... It was always going to come to this.

"Very well, then." She knows she has all she needs. She doesn't need a victim, doesn't need a witness. She is his superior. "I hope you're happy now," she tells him. "I hope your honor's satisfied. Tomorrow, you will go to the Kardoli front. You will die there, fighting terrible men. Like you."

Some time later, the woman who seduced him is walking through the market in the early morning with her children. The twelve-year-old is turning into a remarkably responsible boy, holding his four-year-old brother by the hand and coaxing him with kind words not to wander off, rather than yanking him. It reminds her of the boy's father. He was a pretty young man from down the road she had begged her mother to trade for because his shoulders seemed wide. But his manhood was lacking and it showed in his genteel approach to her.

Her daughter's father was better. Still not much to look at, mind you, but of a significantly greater verve. He had a frenetic energy about him that, unfortunately, seems to have proven hereditary. Now, that girl, her only daughter, who is eight, is tearing the marketplace to shreds. Most of the shopkeepers are accustomed to her and know to watch out for each other when she's around, in case her mother can't, but it's troubling to her the aggression, ambition and even malice she displays. At home, she is always ordering her brothers around, which is as it should be, but when they act out or talk back, she is quick to anger. And when she is alone, it's even more disturbing to watch her exploring outside and hunting for monsters (Where did she even get that idea?) and refusing to even play with her dolls, expressing no interest in caring for the young whatsoever. If she were to grow up barren — perish the thought! — she might become a very good officer indeed, but as a mother, she keeps hoping her daughter will come to find her place in the world as a nurturer and caretaker. As a woman, she is ashamed to be prouder of her sons than her daughter.

Now, her daughter has picked up a rock and brandishes it at the younger brother. "I told you," she says, "to stop following me!" and the four-year-old cries when she lifts it, but her older brother catches her hand and pries the rock out of it, gentle but firm, talking her down from her rage. Then all at once, their mother, having caught the brief exchange out of the corner of her eye, is slow to react to it because she feels a sudden, sharp pain in her belly that makes her feel oddly queasy. At first, she thinks she's physicalizing her worry and disgust at her daughter's behavior, but something tells her no, this is something else. Familiar, but...

She leaves her oldest in charge, telling him to head for a shop owner they all know and love, and she goes to relieve herself. On the way, she starts to wonder, *Is it possible?* She counts on her fingers, trying to keep track of her cycles — how long has it been?

But then who would be the father? Who could it be? By now, the lighthouse encounter she had with the soldier is more than a little bit hazy. She's pushed it to the back of her mind, not because it was disappointing (it

certainly wasn't) or even because it makes her ashamed to think about (though it does, somewhat), she's just had other things on her mind, other people worrying at her. It was a magical encounter, but wasn't meant to be a meaningful one, and she's almost embarrassed to think that she wasn't even considering the thought that she might become pregnant.

She had taken precautions, of course. She always does. But then nothing is entirely certain, so it's not inconceivable. So to speak.

Not that she has anything to fear, though. She's had three children already without too much difficulty, and they've brought her nothing but prosperity and respect. People love mothers and children. The only cause for alarm would be the fact that the child's father happens to be someone who kills people for a living... It makes her shudder, but who will ever know? Who would ever need to?

They have more than enough servants, and she has sampled them often enough. Her mother has always made sure she was invited to the interviews for just that reason. Any one of them would be honored, no doubt, to be acknowledged as sire to even an accidental scion of hers. She knows just which one to go with, too. And she'll have a fourth little bundle of joy in the offing, showering her with glory.

In the years that follow, the soldier takes up arms in defense of his country.

Outside the Bay area, there are monsters who call themselves men and don't obey the commands of their women. They act without consequence. They indulge in anger and in lust for no other reason, it seems, than to... what?

The soldier doesn't even know. Not really. Not for sure. None of them do, these warriors of the Bay of Cats. Beyond their shores, men's appetites are insatiable, but they don't just want food. Women are kept as slaves, as cattle, broodmares for growing more soldiers. Men take them as they please. It makes him sick. Who would even want a woman if she wasn't willing? Where would even be the pleasure in that? Without any connection?

Not that he's been with a woman in years. Not since that night—or the day after, anyway. And that's fine. The officers, they either know how to behave themselves here, or they just don't take a liking to him. And as for the villagers, he knows how to behave around them so as not to attract unwanted attention. He doesn't crave that type of fulfillment. He has better things to worry about—like the men who do.

He has become quite good at killing them. Somewhat of a legend. People ask him why—what makes him so good at killing other men? He tells them it's because they make him sick, that he can't even stand to look at them, he just wants to murder them on sight. He has branded himself a monster against monsters.

But that is not the real reason.

One day, he meets a stranger on the battlefield. The man is wounded and the soldier cannot bring himself to put him out of his misery. Not yet. Not like this. The man is bleeding from the abdomen. It will take him hours to die. But perhaps some part of him can still be saved.

"You're one of them, aren't you?" says the stranger. "From the Bay of Cats? Tell me, does some woman have your balls in a jar back home?"

The soldier doesn't react. The very image is repulsive, but it's beside the point. He detects a game. He doesn't know for sure, but he expects the rules are similar to the games men play back home.

"You Geldirians," the man continues. "You're not men. A man takes what's his. A man takes control of his situation. He doesn't let a woman tell him what to do."

"And what *is* 'his'?" asks the soldier. "What is yours?"

"Everything," says the stranger. Still bleeding, he props himself up on his elbows. "If a man wants a woman, why shouldn't he have her?"

"And why should a man want a woman?" asks the soldier, already knowing whatever game the other man plays, he is losing.

The enemy only laughs through the blood in his lungs. "Do you really need your enemy to explain it to you?"

He doesn't, of course, but again, that's beside the point. There is more to love than sex, and his enemy had just proven that he didn't understand that. And there is also more to sex than love. "She could get pregnant," says the soldier. "Pregnancy can be dangerous."

"So what if she does? It's not my problem! Not unless she's my wife, and I want the child."

A factor that the soldier had never even considered. A wife? He was familiar with the term, vaguely. But that a man should have a say in a child's existence? "What if your wife had another man? And the child wasn't yours?"

"My wife with another man?" At this, the stranger foams at the mouth. "I'd kill her. I would snap her neck, and the child's. I would strangle it in its own adulterous cord! I would— "

The stranger stops speaking because he has what he wanted: the soldier has run his sword through his heart.

The man was bleeding from his abdomen, it would have taken him hours to die.

The soldier senses that whatever game his enemy played, he has now lost by killing him. This makes some sense, considering. But is that what's important?

Killing him was a mercy, but that isn't why the soldier did it. The hate that filled the stranger's words, the cruelty that men can inflict upon women, all the casual atrocity that exists outside the Bay of Cats erupted in the stranger's words, and in a single stroke, the soldier extinguished them. It killed him, too. It absolutely killed him to do it. He would much rather make the world a better place than kill.

But there are worse fates.

One day, more years later still, the woman walks her youngest daughter up the big hill that overlooks the City. It's a wonderful view—of the buildings, of the harbor, the horizons. This child has shown an interest in all things beautiful and sweet and her mother has great hopes she'll be an artist one day and write poems and paint portraits and draw up plans for monumental buildings and see they get made.

But at the top of the hill, they meet a man sitting under a tree.

He recognizes her and he notices that it takes her a moment to recognize him. It takes her just long enough that the daughter becomes curious about him. She is, perhaps, some four years old, and introduces herself and asks the man why he has come here. "For beauty," he says, and then he looks from the girl to her mother. "And maybe for love."

And that's when it hits her. He can see it in her eyes. He has more of a beard now, and his hair—but those shoulders...

"I thought men didn't know about love," says the daughter.

The mother scoffs. "What in the world gave you that idea?"

But before the girl can embarrass her mother further, the man leans over and tells her "Everyone knows about love. But sometimes, we only know the love that we're given. The love that we're shown. Do you know love?"

"Of course!" says the daughter.

"Well, how?"

"Because my mother taught me!"

There's something sullen in his smile, but he puts out a finger and the girl lets him boop her on the nose and then giggles when he says "Boop!" Then he turns back to her mother and sees the tears in her eyes. "Your mother must be a very good teacher," he says.

Before skipping back down the hill, his daughter gives him a flower and a kiss on the cheek and her mother gives a cautious smile. She knows what just happened. She knows what she did, but that's fine. He forgives her. He will never be a father to that little girl in any way she will recall, but that's fine, too. As long as she's happy.

And she can be happy, here. And so can he. The worst thing that could ever happen to a man in his society happened to him. And while his fate, to spend his life ending others', was worse, to him, than death, it still pales in comparison to the fate that befalls women on a daily basis in the patriarchies outside the Bay of Cats.

Spoiler Alert

Alexandra Hara

Alex was raised in Hawaii and has been living in Washington for three years. In addition to writing various forms of creative fiction, she dabbles in poetry, screenwriting, webcomics, cosplay and acting. She holds a BA in English from the University of Hawaii at Manoa and was an intern for the Hawaii Book and Music Festival in 2012. Alex has been writing since the age of seven and has no plans to stop.

There is a love so powerful it can save lives. It can show you the path you're meant to tread, but not everyone is strong enough to walk it. Are you?

In the beginning, there is only the dark.

FADE IN

INT. MESSY STUDIO APARTMENT - NIGHT

The camera pans away with a jerky fumble. For an instant, there is brilliant light that bleaches everything. When the picture clears, a young man appears framed by a cellphone camera in a jerky, tilted angle.

YOUNG MAN: I've decided this is going to be a 'don't you hate it when' video.

He looks like he hasn't slept in days. His dark brown skin is darker beneath his eyes. His black hair is too reflective, unwashed.

YOUNG MAN: So, redshirts.

The camera jumps again and the angle stabilizes. A harsh rattle drowns out the steady, asymmetrical squeak of an old ceiling fan for a second as he puts the phone down at eye level. His palms eclipse the image and he reappears when they part, like a magician revealing a trick.

YOUNG MAN: Like, Star Trek redshirts. (*Thin hands scrub over his face. He drags them down his forehead and cheeks, twisting his features into an exasperated mask. When everything snaps back into place, he's looking skyward.*) Ever since the 2009 reboot, everyone and their mother knows what a redshirt is. Online, at least. "Being a redshirt" has become pretty much, what's the word. (*His eyes search for the missing word in the corner of his room. For two seconds. He gives up.*) The same thing as being expendable, or basically dead meat. Right?

He pushes back from the shot. A tiny studio apartment shifts into focus around him: beige walls, posters held up with temporary mounting putty. A Firefly print droops at one corner, a simple fix neglected. He moves back in close,

blocking out the room behind him with an extreme close-up of his exhausted face.

YOUNG MAN: Thing is, there's a reason these bastards die more often, yeah? Let's forget for a second that Engineering sports the red duds too. Let's focus on the rest of these redshirt guys and gals who tag along on away missions. Only to get shot full of holes or eaten by the monster of the week. They're there because they're a part of the Security and Tactical Division. You know—a dangerous gig. In short, there's a reason they get it. It's not random.

FADE OUT

FADE IN

In the infinite space between frames, anything could have happened—but for all appearances, nothing did.

YOUNG MAN: Sorry, back. What was I saying? Redshirts? Reddit, actually, Jesus, you mention some little bit of trivia about the Security and Tactical Division, try to start a discussion about why redshirts always die first, and suddenly you "must be a lot of fun at parties." Internet, am I right? (*He stares to the left for half a minute, not seeming to mind the dead space in the recording where nothing interesting happens.*) It's cool, though. People don't really get my humor. God, that sounds 3 edgy 5 you, but I mean it. One time I said I was a cliché superhero origin story waiting to happen, my lab partner goes, why, and I said I already had the "dead mom" box checked. (*He pauses.*) I guess that's not funny.

He's smiling for the first time since the video began, but it can only be classified as a smile based on its core ingredients. One side of the mouth quirked slightly up; other, darker things rule the rest of his face.

YOUNG MAN: Whatever, though. Least of my problems, huh? (*He pauses, huffs a laugh.*) Sorry for vague-booking you, random girl who I can only assume will watch this one day. I guess that's pretty dick.

FADE OUT

YOUNG MAN: I'm Elmo, by the way. Please don't ask.

FADE IN

INT. MESSY STUDIO APARTMENT - NIGHT

The camera is held out at arm's length. It cants to the left, then the right. He looks back at it several times, checking that he's still in the frame. During one of his checks his knee collides with an empty hamper and sends it crashing to the floor. Its clattering progress is stopped when it hits a soft pile of laundry that never made it to Point B.

ELMO: (*He rubs his knee.*) Yep. Can't see everything, I guess.

Take-out boxes cohabitate with half-heartedly smashed two-liter bottles of soda. They cede territory only to a tiny folding table with a banged-up Chromebook taking up not enough of its surface space.

ELMO: I day trade. (*He points at the Chromebook.*) I kind of like staying in. That works. You've got to get up at stupid early o'clock to do it, though.

He glances back at the camera, dark eyes flashing for the first time with something more than sarcastic weariness. For just a second, his brows pinch and someone younger peers out from his face.

ELMO: I mean, I don't know why I'm trying to pitch day trading to you. You seem like one of those exhausting social media junkies who actually sees most of their Friends List in person. (*He tilts his head to the side and arches an eyebrow.*) I mean it, you make being a shut-in seem awfully cozy and relaxing. Thanks for making me feel better about this whole situation. (*He gestures behind him at his messy studio.*)

He lets dead space sneak into the recording again. Just the back of his dark, tousled hair is visible, the phone moving up and down gently with his breathing. When he turns back to the camera, the younger him that had peered out from his face earlier is gone.

ELMO: So, grand tour. Office, pathetic pile of month-old laundry... (*He pans the camera.*) cactus, which is the only thing that thrives off pure neglect so, you know, the only thing I can keep alive. (*The shot flashes at a dark patch on the ceiling.*) Probably toxic mold, also something I can keep alive through pure neglect. Is it technically really suicide if you die from something preventable because you're not motivated enough to clear a path for maintenance to come fix something?

He pans around the apartment seven times to catch everything. His never-used vacuum. The one and only Trader Joe's bag he's ever owned, now serving as an honorary trash can. Seven USB drives for seven long-lost wireless mice.

The only thing he does not stop on is a colorful pile of well-worn but meticulously clean leather notebooks. They sit stacked atop his single bookshelf like a peace offering for the vengeful gods of a mountaintop.

ELMO: Anyway, I gotta go. Tomorrow the internet's gonna disappear and I'm gonna have to spend all day on the phone getting it back. (*He rolls his eyes, rasps his thumb across the phone's built-in microphone as he holds it up higher.*) Protip. Don't get a job where the internet is literally the only way you get your paycheck. Not that I think a person like you would, but... just saying. (*He pauses again, then quirks an awkward not-quite-smile.*) Peace.

FADE OUT

Once again, there is only the dark.

ABSOLUTE DARK

ELMO: I have a headache.

The squeak of the ceiling fan; a dull, electric hum from somewhere farther away. If tension had a sound, it would be the loudest one in the room.

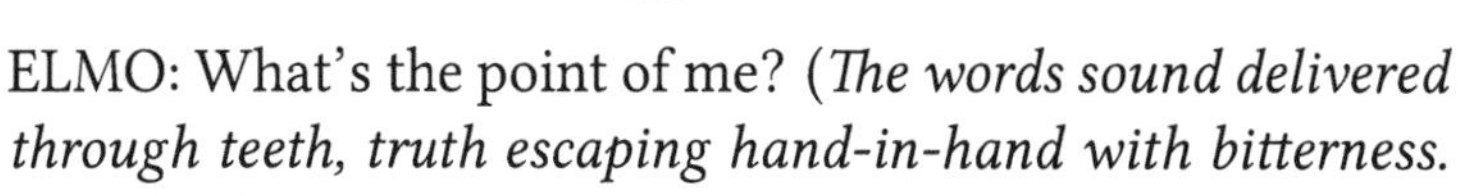

ELMO: What's the point of me? (*The words sound delivered through teeth, truth escaping hand-in-hand with bitterness. Huddled between them, hidden, is sorrow.*) What's the point of this?

There is just the off-kilter squeak of the ceiling fan, the electric hum. Then a ragged sigh, delivered in broken pieces.

ELMO: I'm done with these.

FADE IN

INT. A DIFFERENT KIND OF DARK - NIGHT

This time the dark has depth, shape. It has dark eyes, catching orange streetlight reflections from between broken blinds. The dark has a face, and a name, and when he speaks, the first thing he says is,

ELMO: Sorry.

The camera looks down from above, struggling to focus on the figure below. Shadows embrace blankets and sheets, which in turn embrace the young man on the threadbare twin bed. The orange light in dark eyes is the brightest thing in the quiet room.

ELMO: Big pileup on the freeway. Seven cars. (*In the silence that follows, the eyes stop shifting. They stare instead at a place beneath the phone, deeper into the ceiling, through it into what lies beyond.*) Three dead.

The rustle of the covers is loud without the barely noticeable ambient noises of the day. He rolls to his side and the camera angle shifts. The world tilts, midnight framed in portrait orientation.

ELMO: I don't even drive. I have no idea how I could have stopped this. (*He's nothing more than a silhouette now, orange prison bars of light slatted behind him.*) I know I'll get some... some flash of insight, or something, later. Ideas. How I could've.

His free hand enters the frame for a second and rubs itself across the dark, vague territory of his face. He is still shrouded, nothing more than flat black in the vague shape of a tired man.

ELMO: For now, all I've got are the people. It's... (*The word cuts off, a breath sucks in. Is held. Is let out, slow.*) It's like a punishment, sometimes. "Hey, you know that girl in the yellow Jeep you couldn't save? She loved techno. Like, an unholy amount. All her friends couldn't stand driving with her. She never let them touch her radio. Now she's gone, and won't it be awkward when they start crying every time they hear Sandstorm by Darude?"

Silence slips back in. Outside, a horn blares, long and loud. Someone shouts, but in a cursory way, an angry aside in a life that gets to keep on going.

ELMO: Tomorrow I'll get the whole, 'how I could have not fucked it up' package. For now, I keep filming these fucking videos for a person I don't even know yet.

He pauses, and as if embarrassed by something, he darts his eyes down and to the side. He avoids looking into the camera like that will somehow prevent him from being seen by whoever will watch this image of his face later.

ELMO: Make no mistake. I really don't know you yet. I know you keep joining more Meetup Groups than you can handle. I know your Gmail is a fucking disaster zone. I know you don't like to wear matching socks. But that doesn't mean I know you.

A frown moves across his face next. He still doesn't look into the camera, but a hand lifts up, bumps the phone for a second on its way to run fingers through his hair. He blows out a slow, slightly shaky breath, and closes his eyes. He keeps them shut while he speaks.

ELMO: I guess I'm just assuming these videos are going to be for you. I started seeing your face more and more, but I still don't know why. And then boom, I have to start filming myself, but who the fuck knows what I'm supposed to say. So I figure I'll ramble about redshirts, because clearly that's my calling, right? Taking pointless cellphone videos of my ugly mug yammering about pointless shit while people die and I can't do shit to stop it. (*Finally he opens his eyes. Exhaustion battles with humor, then shakes its hand and shares its space in his eyes.*) It feels like it's okay to say this stuff, for some reason, to you. Whoever you are.

The angle changes. He lays the phone down, and it records the orange beams of light across the ceiling instead. They stretch like roads into the distance, so close and personal at first, then smaller, then pinpoints, then nothing.

ELMO: You know what sucks? Seeing you more and more and having no idea why. Having to wait, to figure out why.

INT. MESSY STUDIO APARTMENT - MORNING

ELMO: Hey.

He doesn't mention anything from the previous night's video. Instead he reheats some day-old coffee, waters his cactus, and gives the camera perched on his microwave a tiny, tired smile.

ELMO: So today I'm going to tell you about how TV Tropes nearly ruined my life.

FADE OUT

FADE IN

INT. MESSY STUDIO APARTMENT - DAY

ELMO: You know what really grinds my gears? The fact that people actually use YKWRGMG instead of just typing or saying "you know what really grinds my gears?" (*He dips his chin and glares a low look of disapproval at the phone, secured now to the top of the Chromebook. His fingers still on its tiny keyboard.*) Also? Who the hell buys a dehumidifier without doing any research whatsoever? You know the brand you bought is absolute garbage, right? It'll be dead in two months. I'm not just saying that, I can actually see that it'll be dead in two months and you'll be all flustered and also have dry, flaky skin. (*His look of judgment struggles hard to smother*

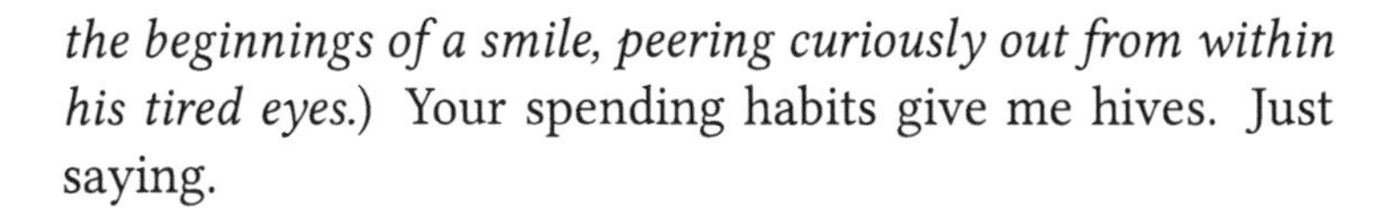

the beginnings of a smile, peering curiously out from within his tired eyes.) Your spending habits give me hives. Just saying.

FADE OUT

FADE IN

INT. MESSY STUDIO APARTMENT - MORNING

ELMO: You know why my parents named me Elmo? (*His black hair is defying gravity, hanging down toward the floor, which is the ceiling to the camera right now. Behind his head a slice of the dark place beneath his bed shares the background with a rumpled white sheet.*) It was this movie from the 80s, St. Elmo's Fire.

With a huff of effort, he rolls upright off the bed. The camera pans in a wild swing, and as he walks across the studio apartment, little changes show the passage of time. A slightly smaller stack of take-out boxes. A pair of running shoes, still in the box, partially obscured by the small Chromebook on the table.

ELMO: Sort of wish I'd been named for the actual St. Elmo's Fire, that... that purplish electric light that happens when sharp things move through a storm. Sailors thought that was good luck. (*He pauses for a thoughtful moment, eyes on something arbitrary while his mind is on something completely different.*) I could get behind that. (*He shrugs.*) But hey, joke's on my folks, because a Sesame Street puppet eclipsed the fuck out of all of that, anyway.

FADE OUT

FADE IN

INT. MESSY STUDIO APARTMENT - DAY

The cellphone camera is secured to the microwave again, showing a slightly diagonal shot of a kitchen disaster. He wrangles a pot of boiling-over noodles while he talks, turning his face away from clouds of occasional steam.

ELMO: Right, remember from the video last Monday, when I said I was pretty sure my neighbor is a hoarder? (*With a grunt of effort, he moves the pot to the sink instead, then turns to peer back at the camera over his shoulder.*) So I have more proof now, it's irrefutable, and I know I said I hate mint chocolate chip ice cream last month but Jesus, I think I might have just had, I don't know, the world's shittiest ice cream all the way up until now? (*He turns back to the pot.*) Aw, shit. (*It is said with an exhale of laughter.*) Maybe that's what I'll have for dinner instead. How the hell do you make noodles and dance to Gangnam Style at the same time next week? Burn the witch.

FADE OUT

The apartment is not the only thing that changes. The bags don't leave his eyes, but they lighten, become less active and more a mark of when his sleep deprivation used to be worse. He laughs, three separate times, once an aborted snort, once a reedy, nervous chuckle, and once a full-bodied guffaw that starts that video off explosively, the camera angle wild, the flashing lights of the ceiling

fan jarring and strange as the explosive stimuli that make up an infant's first day.

He has a passion for horrible Dad jokes and unwieldy acronyms. He tacks on internetisms to his rambling speeches: unpopular opinion, TL;DR, spoiler alert.

The videos come every day for nearly three months. Eighty-eight recordings, the shortest barely half a minute long, the longest over an hour.

And then the videos stop.

FADE IN

INT. MESSY STUDIO APARTMENT - NIGHT

The light has changed when the next video starts. The pale, strained sun of early spring has given way and bloomed into a full, slow, sticky summer. The voice comes from off camera.

ELMO: Sorry.

The subtle, mounting changes from earlier videos are gone. The mess is back, spilling out into the neglected workstation. Piles of printed computer sheets take up most of the bed, and the comforter is packed down onto the computer chair in a makeshift nest. The Firefly poster has finally fallen, or else been taken down by choice.

In its place are sticky notes and index cards thumb tacked into rental walls with no care for the damages or the security deposit. They are too far away for the camera to focus on, but messy block letters cover every available surface.

ELMO: It's been kind of a bit. I know... now, anyway, that you don't like it when people feel like they need to make excuses for things like that. When they go off the grid, I mean. So... I guess I won't make up excuses.

He still hasn't entered the frame. There is a shadow on the far wall, dark and crisp, cast in bold and unafraid contrast by the strengthened sun.

ELMO: I figure I might as well keep up with these. I stopped for a bit, shit got too real. But, at this point? I sort of just want to talk to you.

The silhouette stops moving, comes into focus. His wrists are thinner, his shoulders sharper.

The fourth laugh he gives the recordings is not a laugh at all. It is the sound of desperation, like breaking glass and a minor key where a major was expected instead.

ELMO: Fuck, I literally just realized my very first one of these videos was about redshirts. Holy shit, does this go way deeper than I ever suspected, or is life just funny that way?

It's the only sign-off he gives as he snags the phone off the table and slams his hand against the screen.

FADE OUT

FADE IN

INT. MESSY STUDIO APARTMENT - NIGHT

ELMO: I'm not a stalker. (*He speaks from behind the bars of his fingers, closed tight over his face.*) That's not a promising way to start this video, I know. I'm sorry. I... am not choosing to be a stalker. It's actually, truly involuntary. (*The hands drop and suddenly dark eyes stare into the camera, like he can substitute a Samsung Galaxy for the person he really wants to address. His dark hair is shiny again. The beard looks several weeks old. The bags under his eyes are so dark it looks like he's been punched.*) And I don't mean that the way people do when they say they're addicted to nicotine or heroin or porn and it's no longer a choice. I mean this is really, completely, honestly, not a choice.

The silence stretches. Inside it is the asymmetrical ceiling fan squeaking overhead, the electric hum. Traffic outside. Tortured, slow breathing, like each one is struggling not to be birthed into the world as the beginning of a panic attack.

ELMO: I know... entirely too much about you. (*Shame steals the thousand-yard stare. Guilt weighs down his head, and the frantic light in his eyes slips behind shutters.*) You were probably curious, all the way up until this point. If I were you, I'd stop watching right now. But I know you'll keep going. (*The words don't sound like a plea, or a declaration of unshakable faith. They sound like a weather report.*) But I also know that now, you're probably scared.

The next breath that comes sounds like the union between a huff of laughter and a stifled sob. He masks it with a wet, painful cough. Lifts his hand from his mouth to press it into his forehead.

ELMO: It's okay. I am, too.

FADE OUT

FADE IN

INT. MESSY STUDIO APARTMENT - NIGHT

He isn't looking at the camera. His eyes are fixed on his steepled fingers, but also through them, and his gaze also never leaves the inside of his own mind. It is flat, and final, and infinite.

ELMO: I don't know what to say. Nothing's working.

The organized towers of printed pages on the bed have turned into piles. The comforter is on the floor, trampled flat. The cactus is gone.

ELMO: Why am I surprised? I shouldn't be surprised. (*His eyes track back and forth for a second, like he's reading a teleprompter but not comprehending what he sees. A grimace interrupts the flat exhaustion on his face for an instant. His eyes track again.*) It just stops. It just stops? So, okay, it just stops. Always fucking there.

When he stands up it seems incidental at first, hands pulled through greasy hair, like he'll wander, maybe relocate to the chair.

Instead he spins, and his arm collides with the stack of pages. They explode like frightened doves, and the sound of his throat tearing on a blood-red scream marries the crash of the chair hitting the wall in a perfect union of chaos. The Chromebook leaves the table, smashes into the far wall. The blinds rattle right by the speaker, catching some other flung object, and the phone is knocked from its place on the table.

Then there is just the dark.

FADE OUT

FADE IN

INT. MESSY STUDIO APARTMENT - NIGHT

He is sitting on the floor at the foot of his bed. The cellphone camera moves with his breathing, held in cupped hands like a wounded animal. He is as small and broken as the shattered apartment around him.

ELMO: I have what-if scenarios. They aren't the same as the rest of the things I see. But I think about them anyway.

His voice is bloody with the rattle of where his screams have torn his throat. He props the phone up on his knees, freeing up his hands. There is the sound of a sheaf of paper sliding across the floor, and then it is in his hands and in the corner in the frame.

ELMO: Like maybe I go on the run. (*He folds a corner down.*) I move, right now. (*Another corner.*) There's not exactly a two-weeks' notice for day trading. I can afford to break my lease.

He now holds a simple paper airplane, grade-school level in design and function. He analyzes it from all angles, presses a shaking finger gently against the sharp nose.

Then he throws it. The little plane vanishes off-camera.

ELMO: But I've tried to outrun them before. And it's never worked.

Another sheaf of paper finds its way into his hands, but he folds this one more carefully. Bitten fingernails smooth out the folds. Angles emerge, aerodynamic, complicated, precise.

ELMO: Or maybe I go and find you. Not that—not that you know any of this. These are all still trapped on my phone, all these... one-sided conversations. These echoes. And you won't know any of this, not a damned thing, not until it's too late for any of it to matter.

The plane is done. The more complex design dips up at the wingtips, more of a jet than a plane. He studies it, runs his fingers along its bottom-most fold. Throws it, too.

ELMO: I'd be just another crazy person ranting at you. Maybe you'd pepper me, I know by now you've started carrying it on your morning run. Don't judge yourself for getting worked up over a self-defense video on YouTube. There are way worse things to obsess about.

He does not fold the third sheet of paper at all. He just holds it, careful and tender, like a page torn from a Bible. Like an old, yellowing birth certificate.

ELMO: But what if I just introduce myself? Start hanging out at that ridiculous free-trade crunchy granola tea shop you like. Just... strike up conversation. Explain how lost I am when it comes to chamomile and ginseng. Maybe we could be friends? If you can stomach my dietary habits.

This pause is the longest. His eyes never lift, no sounds of folding paper interrupt the strange, perfect silence of the room.

ELMO: (*He chuckles.*) It feels like I should expand on that here, but I'm actually really not that creative. The things I see... I don't cook any of it up myself. I've got pretty much no imagination. (*The paper in his lap rustles, but he still does not fold it.*) Sometimes I wonder if that's why I'm so bad at this. Why I've failed so much.

He flips it over in his hands, once, then another time. He doesn't stop, turning it slowly, until it sounds like a single wing struggling for flight, a paper heartbeat.

ELMO: But if I said, "fuck it," avoided wearing red for the rest of my life, found you, ordered some kind of artisanal coffee and gagged it down to break the ice? If we did become friends?

The paper stops. For a long time, so does he.

ELMO: I'd like that.

And here is the longest silence of all. A ten-minute stretch of nothing, the ceiling fan broken and silent, the traffic sounds muffled from where he still sits insulated from the outside world on the ground at the foot of his bed. The paper is still, the phone is still, and he is still. His eyes do not track, left and right, as if reading a teleprompter. They stare, but his gaze never makes it past his own mind.

ELMO: But I can't. I can't choose what I want over those people.

The sound of the paper crumpling in his fist is deafening after all that silence, after his quiet words. He throws the balled-up sheet away, and his eyes follow it, and then slip past it, through it again.

ELMO: There are so many people.

FADE OUT

THE RETURN OF THE ABSOLUTE DARK

ELMO: It isn't going to be your fault, but you'll feel like it is anyway.

I could give you a detailed explanation of all the factors that lead up to the accident tomorrow. There are dozens of little things, and behind each of those things, dozens more. Low tire pressure. A GPS interruption because someone forgot to turn off a reminder on her phone. This leads to that, which leads to that, which leads to that. Maybe it'll help you understand that sometimes life just does this.

These aren't bad people. It's not malicious, no more than your role in what happens is malicious. The first driver meant to get his tires filled this weekend. Isn't that always how it goes when you have a bad blowout? The second driver never checks her phone when she drives, never. She's one of those bleeding hearts who cries at Hallmark commercials, cries at those distracted driving PSAs. The GPS screw-up thing will be the first and last time she ever looks down at her phone while she's on the road. And you, the third driver, didn't do anything wrong except slam on your brakes to stop from hitting the cars in front of you. You didn't mean to lose control. You didn't mean to swerve off the road.

I get it if you're mad at me now. I can't see it—it's weird. It's the only thing I can't see now, so close to the end.

You might be wondering why I don't stop it. I don't know, maybe you think I'm melodramatic, or sadistic. Maybe you think I want this big, meaningful death, and I don't care if it puts you through hell, so I don't stop it.

But I don't want to die. I promise you, I swear to you, I don't want to die.

And I don't want you to hate yourself about tomorrow.

FADE IN

EXT. THE LAST BEAUTIFUL DAY OF SUMMER

Sunlight streams in through the gaps in leaves that are just starting to blush red, leaves that don't yet know their days are numbered.

Elmo's shirt is redder than any of the foliage. Though it is the first recording filmed outside his apartment, though he again looks like he hasn't slept in months, his eyes are bright. He is awake, alert, and there is a stillness and calm in the steady dark gaze he points down at his phone.

ELMO: You're going to get my power. It's how this works.

He can't decide where to look. One second he's drinking in the sun, staring into it too long, so long his eyes stream. Then he's looking back to his phone, like he doesn't want to look away from eyes that will see this in the future. Then a tree will slow his feet, drag his gaze away, and when he looks back to the camera, emotion has made a masterpiece of his tired features.

ELMO: I killed my mother, before I even took my first breath of this—this fucking amazing, fresh, perfect air. (*He breathes deep, lets it out shakily. He does not cry.*) When she died, I got her sight, her ability to see what you're going to start seeing. It's how this passes along. She... Mom saw I was going to kill her, I think. Saw it before she even made the choice to get pregnant with me. She never outright said it in any of the journals she left behind, but... I think I know. I feel like I know. I—

He cuts himself off, breathes deep again, three times, fast and full. Winces, puts a hand to his forehead.

ELMO: I know how hard it is, learning how to use the sight, trying to get it right when all you've got are the words of someone who's already gone. Mom was better at it. Her journals are yours now. I've arranged to have them mailed to you. And a password on an index card in the front cover of the red book. Gotta love Cloud sharing sites. Try not to judge me for the username and password. I was... extremely seventeen when I made them.

He cracks a smile down at the phone, the kind of smile that someone who loves him would want to play over and over and over after he's gone, after it stops being too painful to see it over and over and over.

ELMO: It's not a good power. It's going to feel like it's wrecking your life. If I could avoid giving it to you, I would.

In the distance, a child screams, but it turns into a shrill, reckless cackle of joy. An older person answers with a lower, more reserved laugh. Elmo looks up, arrested by the sound for a long breath of a moment.

ELMO: But here's the thing. (*He doesn't look at the phone. His eyes are still in the distance, with the playing strangers, past the confines of his mind and perfectly present.*) You're going to be amazing at it. It's the one thing that comforts me, now.

The sounds of a busier main drag filter in, background noise that is easy to ignore at first. Then less so.

ELMO: So many people. (*His voice is tighter now, his breaths come a little faster.*) You're going to help so many people. I could never really get it, and it will be hard for you, but you will get it. It's so clear to me now.

For thirty seconds, Elmo stops at the intersection that crosses the world of the laughing child and the world of screaming tires. He breathes, eleven times, eyes closed, tired face turned to the sun.

ELMO: You'll do better than I did.

He glances back down at the phone, holds it up for a better angle of the peaceful stretch of road behind him, the path lined with trees that don't yet know they're dying. In the end, his grin is free of fear.

ELMO: Spoiler alert.

And everything returns to the dark.

FADE OUT

From Lullabies to Love Songs and Funeral Dirges

Alan Streeter

Alan Streeter began to write as a hobby one year before his retirement from the Pharmaceutical Industry. Having an eclectic nature, he was also a Documentary Photographer for over seven years and earned his MFA in Photography at the University of Arizona, where he also taught Beginning Photography. He later served in the U.S. Army as a Commissioned Officer and Aviator. Achieving the rank of Captain and status of Flight Commander. He has recently completed his first novel, Brightness.

Love doesn't just mean different things to different people. Even for one person, it can change over time, and if we spend our lifetime pondering its meaning–well, we should be so lucky.

I can still remember how we bounded up the brick stairs, and how the raindrops' kisses on my forehead made me blink. I could leap two or more steps at a time, so I grinned and pulled harder, urging my hands to not lose hold of my mother's and father's grasp, as we skipped to the top.

Skating through the front door on slippery soles, I was welcomed by the organ's haunting embrace as the melody floated through the walls and floorboards of this grand church. The soothing warmth of the furnace greeted me along with everyone crossing the arched threshold this Sunday morn. The vestibule was crowded with parishioners lining up to check their coats, or waiting for partners to return from the restrooms before being ushered to the pews. There were many among the whispering flock who were more concerned with the latest gossip about him and her, or them, rather than some trivial pursuit of repenting their sins and praying for God's forgiveness, as my mother would say.

The redolent crush of perfumes, colognes and lotions that preceded the old ladies and men brushing past hung heavy. Their aroma danced around my nose, threatening to overwhelm me. My throat reflexively cut off the smells before they went all the way down to my churning stomach. The very fact I didn't lose my breakfast of champions, right there and then would be one more addition to my long and growing list of "Wonders of the World".

My attention quickly settled elsewhere while Mom tugged at my overcoat and I was much too busy looking around to assist her. There was a tension in the air as she got my coat off and now hurriedly struggled with her own. There was some sort of timer about such things kids like me were not made aware of. My father, having cast off his heavy topcoat with only a shrug and slight arch of his back, was now waiting. He may have been holding the timer. I wasn't sure. What I did know was, the way he took off his coat was a great trick. How was he able to do that?

It was also a wonder how the old man at the coat check counter could see around the stack of coats handed to him. But he didn't miss a step as he turned with his bundle and placed them one by one on hangers, removing the numbered chips from each one and when all three were hung, ambled back to the counter to hand my father the claim checks. The old man smiled at him then and turned his eyes slowly over to my mother, where they stopped, waiting for her to catch his gaze. When she did, he smiled again, broad and ever so sweetly. He gave me only the briefest of "How ya doing, kid?" nods and moved on. So did I.

There were always those among us longing for glances and smiles from my parents. We were endlessly greeted with the kindest of hellos. Folks clamored to shake my father's hand and to kiss my mother's cheek. My parents were magnets, drawing all sorts of rusty ferrous metals to their poles. There was no mystery to this attraction. To see them made you want to be near them. Simply stated, my parents were beautiful. Stunning, as a matter of fact. And even now, as a man very much older than the couple occupying my recollection with dog-eared photographs and memories, that conclusion remains. My mother and father were the absolute ideal of a happy, loving couple.

From an early age, I delighted in accompanying my mother to the grocery store, to the laundromat, or shopping Downtown. The strange thing was, Mom didn't appear to notice the stares. The way bag boys would push and wrestle each other out of the way for the opportunity to bag her canned goods. But what remained a Wonder of the World was how they melted with just a smile from Mother's lips. I was proud she was my mother and that I received the love and affection from someone so adored.

Even years past the necessity to hold her hand when crossing the street, I'd grab for it to make clear to any passing car's occupant, she was my mom.

I was a child of the Sixties and therefore often placed in the loving care of our electronic au pair, a twenty-three-inch RCA Victor television set. It became clear that although Mom might have looked a lot like the mothers on my favorite TV Shows – *Father Knows Best* and *Leave it to Beaver* – our home life was different in many fundamental ways. My father didn't always make it home for dinner and that upset Mom. I had never noticed June Cleaver scold Ward for being late to dinner. But my mom sure did.

"Where the hell have you been?" she whispered when I walked down the hall, presumably out of earshot.

"You know damn well where I've been, so stop asking. I went to have a few beers before coming home. Is that all right with you?" my father replied, not unkindly.

"A few? Huh... A few dozen would be closer, judging by how you smell."

How he smelled? I'd have to remember to take a good whiff when I went back to the kitchen.

"Okay... Sweetheart... You can get off my back now."

"I would just love it if, at the very least, you would call me to say you'll be coming home late. Can you do that?"

"I don't see what the big deal is, but if it will make you feel better, I'll try to remember to do so."

Well, that answer sounded to my ears to be nice. They were getting back to their loving selves again.

I couldn't recall what toy I'd gone to my room to retrieve, so I picked up my baseball glove sitting on the shelf and returned to the front of the house. Seeing my

mom and dad there in the kitchen, Dad helping with putting away dishes he hadn't been around to dirty, they looked okay, happy. As I walked past the kitchen door, my dad saw me and said, "Hey Little Buddy, how was your day?"

"Okay, I guess."

"Any homework?"

"No... Second Graders don't have homework," I said with a frown. Punching the hollow of the glove's palm.

"Ha, I guess you're right. Well, love ya, Son."

"Love you, Dad."

I stopped momentarily, and there it came, the reason for my pause.

"Love ya, Son." This time from my mother.

"Love you too, Mom." I continued to the living room. Sadly, my baseball glove lacked use and was much too stiff to fold. *Gilligan's Island* was on, so I set my glove aside and focused on the show, shutting out the whispered conversation my parents were having.

Turned out, it was an episode I had seen before. So my mind drifted and soon set sail. I found myself lost on my own deserted isle. I wondered—were Mr. Howell and Lovey in love? And if so, did they ever argue? Did Mr. Howell ever come home late for dinner? Did Mrs. Howell care? And what about, what about... the Professor and Mary Ann? Were they married? For a while, I thought there might be something going on between Gilligan and Mary Ann (maybe she wasn't married to the Professor after all), but he always fouled it up somehow. I felt kind of sorry for Gilligan. Especially because at times he reminded me of... well... me. A six-and-a-half-year-old version of the Skipper's Little Buddy.

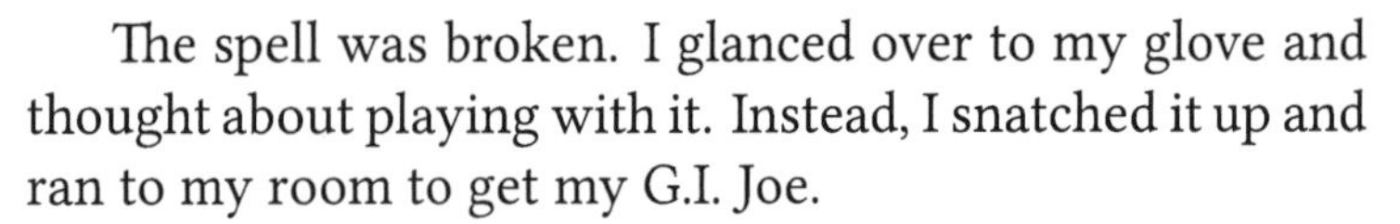

The spell was broken. I glanced over to my glove and thought about playing with it. Instead, I snatched it up and ran to my room to get my G.I. Joe.

Did I mention how I loved it when my mother would come to school for Parent-Teacher Day? My friends and teachers would talk about it for days afterward.

"Gee, your mom's so pretty," the girls would say. And others would announce, "I wish she were my mom." Some of the less gracious would conclude, "She's not your mom," or "How could she have such a goon for a son?"

Unfortunately, I took both compliment to her and criticism to me equally. But it was when the teachers would speak out, that I was most struck with pride. They were like the folks at church. Always happy to see her. Always spending far more time than what was normally spent with other kids' parents. Lavishing their praises, complimenting my feistiness and congratulating her on what a fine job she and my father were doing raising me. And it was funny how almost every lady teacher found a way during the conversation to ask if my father would be attending the next Parent-Teacher meeting in the Spring? As time moved on and as some of the Wonders of the World began to be explained, I started to understand there was something self-serving about those questions. Something unkind.

Seemed like as soon as you get a thing figured out, something else comes in to mess it all up. And that's what happened late one night. I remember waking up the following morning with the hope I had just dreamed it. But after seeing Mom with her sunglasses on in the

kitchen, dressed in her bathrobe, I knew things had changed.

I awoke to a thud, a crash, a hiss, a scream. Funny how they all seemed to occur at the same time. Another thing I remember is how *awake* I was. I was wide awake and sitting straight up in my bed, listening, shivering, and there it was again. This time in reverse of what I thought I had heard before. There was a scream, "No, Eric...", a hiss, "You whining bitch!", a crash, sounded like a lamp. *Could it be the TV?* And a thud. *What?* I got out of bed to see.

The space between the foot of my bed and the door was about five feet, but that night it felt like fifty. I cracked open the door, just a little, and listened, bending my ears to pick up anything. Nothing was heard. I opened the door wider, but still couldn't see a thing. I couldn't feel a thing, although it may have been a bit colder. And I couldn't smell a thing. On second thought, maybe I could still smell the hamburger Mom had made for her and me after Dad had not made it home again for...

I had covered the length of the hallway while taking into account the reports from my four outward facing senses. At the end of the hall to the left was the living room. The TV was upright and nothing appeared out of place. To my right, the kitchen. There I saw my mother in the corner, hands over her face, sobbing as I had never heard anyone cry before. It was a Wonder of the World, I didn't run to her then. I may have made some noise because she took her hands away from her face and looked first in my direction and then with greater trepidation back into the kitchen towards a place in the room blocked from my view. The look on her face was terrifying. *What's happening?* I rushed to enter the room and she screamed, "No!"

I froze.

"Go, go. Get out of here, get out... of... Go back to your room."

I didn't move. I couldn't. My legs refusing my mother's command.

She looked once again to the place in the room I couldn't see. I moved. Not away but towards the kitchen. When she realized I wasn't retreating, Mom rose to her feet and ran in the direction of whatever was just around the corner. *Is it a monster?* I had to see it.

Time slowed. What would have taken a second, stretched into tens of seconds, minutes, and suddenly my mother flew backward across the room, (*There* was *a monster!*) her hip smashing against the counter next to the stove, and moving towards her was... my father. He lunged at her, but my mom looked only at me.

"Get out! Please... Son, now. Go to your room!"

Time snapped back to real time, and there were those sounds again: A thud, a crash, a hiss and a scream. Their once enigmatic origins were now perfectly clear. I ran back to my room.

Slamming the bedroom door closed behind me, I went to the closet and crawled behind the hanging clothes. Pushing aside the shoes haphazardly assembled in rows of twos and threes on the floor and from the edge of the closet, from the deep corners, I pulled down the hardly-ever-worn, oversized, and undersized pieces of clothing hanging there and began to construct my fortress.

Unfortunately, my makeshift stronghold wasn't sound proof. The noises continued through the night. They swept from one end of the house to the other. Erupting in the living room and next in the bathroom across from my room, and so on.

My means of greater protection was to build my fort taller. I convinced myself that I was now completely hidden underneath an innocuous, albeit misadventured, naturally formed mound of fallen clothes and shoes, in the back of my bedroom closet, invisible to anyone who may come looking. It was a Wonder of the World no one came into my room that night and even more puzzling, how I was able to fall asleep.

I awoke to blades of light cutting through the hinged edge of the closet door. Did I mention it was the weekend? Saturday, as a matter of fact, and given the recent arrival of our first color TV, the call of Saturday morning cartoons was strong. *But what about last night? Is Mom all right?* Was it all a dream? Attempting to piece together the events of the previous night wasn't easy. Sleep didn't want to release the compassionate hold it had on me. Groggily, I rubbed my eyes, which were sore for some reason, and replaced my pillow—a shoe—with a pair of pants. I reached behind to remove the other tenner shoe from the small of my back. Then I opened the other eye and scanned the space. *All clear.*

Suddenly, I was fully awake and heard those sounds again. *Will it never end?* I felt shell-shocked, weary. I couldn't remember being this tired. The sounds skidded through my head, bouncing from one side to the other and slowly, I came to realize I was imagining them. They were only in my head. *Only in my head?*

But what wasn't my imagination was the faint smell of bacon in the air. Being overcome with the urgent call of Saturday morning cartoons, to having to go to the bathroom, and now the groaning of my stomach, I pushed myself up and out of the closet. I walked over to the bedroom door and pressed my head against it, listening for any warning sound. Nothing. I opened the door. It looked like it was going to be a pretty day. Light was hitting all of the spots normally touched when the morning sun was making a big show of things outdoors. There was no movement I could sense. But the undeniable aroma of frying bacon permeated the hallway.

And I heard it: a sizzling, followed by the sound of the refrigerator door being closed and eggs being tap-tap-tapped on the side of a skillet and the unmistakable pop and sizzle, as the yolks slid onto the hot bacon grease.

Walking down the hall towards those amiable sounds, I had almost convinced myself last night was just a dream, then I saw her. My mother, standing over the kitchen stove, her cigarette cantilevered on the edge of the counter, burning lazily down to a butt. She had her bathrobe on, which wasn't an odd sight for a Saturday morning breakfast. What made it strange was, she had her sunglasses on.

Just as I began to wonder about that, she turned to me. For a moment, the muscles of her face went still and we stared at each other. Then she reached up, adjusted her sunglasses, covering the blue smudge under her eyebrow and said, in a hoarse voice, "Good morning, Son."

"Morning, Mom. Can I watch cartoons?"

"Yes, but not for too long. Breakfast will be ready soon."

"Oh... ah, OK. Thanks." I turned towards the living room.

"Love ya, Son."

I stopped in my tracks. For the first time in my life, that sentence sounded strangely discordant. I was confused. It was a wonder I didn't start to bawl right there and then. I looked back to my mother, but she'd returned her attention to the eggs.

"Love you, too, Mom," was all I could think to say as a reply and started once again towards the living room, and to my cartoons.

As I look back, I realize monsters really did exist in my world, and the lullabies had ended. I realize how that moment defined for me the unfairness of love, its aloofness and mystery. What was this thing? It was becoming obvious that real love didn't exist between my mother and father. I had missed that call. It was clearly a strike and not a ball. I questioned if love had ever existed between them. I started questioning if I had a clue of what love was. Life owed me a thorough explanation and it was a Wonder of the World how long it took to get one.

I didn't see much of my father after that night. The facade of Mom and Dad's marriage had crumbled completely and irreparably. But for some reason, I kept the fort in my bedroom closet, just in case.

Then a funny thing happened: I grew older. And my obsession with defining love and affection grew all the more intense. Movies and songs began to fulfill their role in establishing the dimensions of this strange affliction. There was puppy love often found in the songs of The Jackson Five, movies and songs of unrequited love, romantic love and passionate love. All types, but I particularly enjoyed films and shows like Zeffirelli's *Romeo and Juliet* and Rodgers and Hammerstein's *Cinderella.* I was enthralled, especially with Cinderella. I won't say how long I had a crush on Lesley Ann Warren, the actress portraying her, but to this day, every couple of years I reach for the VHS on the shelf of prehistoric tapes and throw it in the VCR.

Romeo and Juliet and *Cinderella* don't have the same effect as before, and I am beguiled by their stories and lyrics to a lesser extent. Perhaps the accumulation of years has muted my emotions with the callus of logic and a numbing intellectual fascination with prose.

During those years after my father's departure, I claimed only two friends; Butch, my dog of Collie/German Shepard mix and Albert, a human boy. Butch was a good listener. Albert was better at talking than listening, but he was okay.

As we walked, a hastening wind hurried down the Sycamore- and Maple-strewn avenue, reanimating the fallen leaves, urging on their impromptu game of Tag. Albert was explaining his new theory of what love was, a topic he too was preoccupied with. "It's a conspiracy!" he rang out, his hands waving in a gesture of excitement and prepubescent awkwardness. "It's a plot perpuated... perputead... perpetuated on the masses to control and distract us from what's really important."

Albert definitely had a way with words, but I wasn't buying it. "What are they trying to distract us from?" I asked calmly, masking my excitement.

"I don't know exactly, but it's got to be something huge. Just look around. It's everywhere on the radio. Listen to Michael, that's all he ever sings about. Listen to the Osmonds. You can't get away from it."

The thing was, much of what Albert was saying made sense to me. He wasn't making up facts. And the more I thought about it, the more examples I could come up with myself. But I still wasn't convinced. "Hey, who's 'they'? Who exactly is in charge of this conspiracy of yours?

Could it be the Mayor, the Congress, the Government?" This was all I had come away with from the social studies class I attended the previous year.

Albert quietly thought about my question. This was a first. Usually, once Albert got going, it was hard to get him to stop. Kinda like a windup toy car I once had. I'd crank the key all the way until I couldn't turn it any more and then let it go. The vehicle would speed across the room, bounce off the opposite wall and head down the hall. It would never stop unless I ran after it and lifted the wheels off of the ground. Albert was a lot like that toy car.

Looking up to a sky filling with cirrus clouds, Albert distractedly pulled a tattered baseball cap over his red-tipped ears to block the chill of a sunset well on its way to dusk. "I don't know," he began, "It could be, but I think it's even bigger than the government."

"What's bigger than the government?" I asked.

He stopped and grinned at me knowingly. "You ask good questions for someone so short."

I was an inch shorter and a year younger than him, and he never let me forget it.

"Maybe it's the church?" he whispered. Well, he sort of whispered. Another thing about Albert when he got wound up like this was his whispers were more akin to mini shouts.

"That makes no sense at all. What did Michael Jackson have to do with the church?" I argued.

"You know he's a Jehovah's Witness."

"Yeah, but I think it's only a coincidence."

We were silent again. This in and of itself was a phenomenon. Two boys quietly contemplating a problem not baseball related? If someone had seen us then looking so grave, thinking so hard, we might have been mistaken for boys much older than we actually were. Boys of a serious nature. But if Butch could speak, he would say we were far from.

"I'm not convinced it's the church," I said, breaking the silence.

"What about all the 'Love Thy Neighbor' stuff? I'm telling you, they're in on it."

I had a feeling this turn in the conversation had taken us down a wrong road. I looked down at Butch laying at my feet. He'd decided to take this opportunity to get some rest. We'd run him pretty hard at the park. Good Ol' Butch was always at my side during these conversations, if not always on my side. And to highlight that point, he raised his eyebrows and looked up at me, blew a little puff of air through his nostrils and sleepily closed his eyes. Seemed like he thought we were going down the wrong road, too.

"Okay, let's think about music again." Albert was desperate to make a U-Turn. "Think about Barry Manilow, Bread, Diana Ross. Think about the Temptations. I dare you to come up with a song ever sung by that group that wasn't a love song. Just try," he challenged with a grin even broader than before.

"Ah... 'Papa Was a Rollin Stone'?" I offered with a smile of my own.

"No way! 'Papa Was a Rollin Stone' is about a family broken apart and the death of their father. It's a love song. Sad, but still a love song."

"Well what about, what about... ah... 'Do Your Ears Hang Low?'"

"Do your... what?"

"You know... *Do your ears hang low? Do they wobble to and fro*?" I quietly sang, feeling a little self-conscious.

"Are you serious? That's stupid. It's a campfire song."

"Yeah, but it's not a love song."

"First: The Temptations have never recorded 'Do Your Ears Hang Low?' and second: I'm not saying there are no non-love songs. I'm just saying, there are more love songs than one could imagine. If you just..."

"Dude, where'd you come up with this anyway?" All of a sudden, Albert didn't sound himself. I was coming to the conclusion this wasn't as original an idea, as he had led me to believe.

"I overheard my uncles talking about it last Thanksgiving between the games," he confided, "One even said he thought it was a drug pushed on us like cocaine. All you needed was a little taste, and you were hooked."

I laughed and Butch opened his eyes. Albert might actually be on to something.

"Holy Cow. A drug!"

Albert nodded. Butch sat up. His ears trying their very best to do the same. He could get the right one to stand, but the left one was broken or something.

This still didn't answer the question of conspiracy or who might truly be perpetuating it. (Come to think of it, maybe Albert meant perpetrating.) Nor had we an answer for what they were keeping us from thinking about. I was nonetheless still intrigued, and there was an idea of my own burning to be shared.

"I didn't want to mention this earlier." I licked my lips. (I always licked my lips when I was nervous.) Cautiously, I continued, "but we have to at least give it consideration. Did you ever think maybe it has something to do with aliens?"

Albert was quiet again and began to stroke his chin in a slow, deliberate way, like his and my favorite villain, "Ming the Merciless". Albert didn't have a beard, but when he did, he wanted to be well practiced. Butch was far less introspective. He breathed in a broad and toothy yawn of disappointment and laid back down. I don't think he agreed with my alien theory at all.

The street lamps started to blink on around us. "Maybe..." As he replied, small smoke signals rose from his lips in the cold. "But I think it is definitely a drug."

"Yeah, like in that *Outer Limits* episode. You know, that really terrifying one with the black rocks," I offered, in an attempt to buttress the integrity of the idea.

"Those rocks weren't drugs, they weren't even rocks."

Standing there, arguing with Albert in the cold made my toes ache. I waved him to start walking again and gave a quick slap on my thigh to get Butch moving as well.

We, although not little kids anymore, weren't interested in drugs. That was another reason why I liked hanging out with Albert. Many of the other older guys just wanted to hide behind their garages and smoke cigarettes stolen from their parents, talking about (lying about) the weed they smoked the previous weekend and how messed up they had been. This wasn't my or Albert's thing.

This dope called Love, though, was something altogether different and I desperately wanted to try it, to taste it. Sad thing was, I became a junkie. A junkie just trying to get a fix and failing miserably to do so.

My failure with romance came so easily, so often, and in the most extravagant of ways. Every clamorous debacle left its fiery brand on my heart. Thank goodness there were never any children involved in the wrecks. Just two adults who should have known better, left to pull themselves out of the debris and deal with what was left in the best way possible.

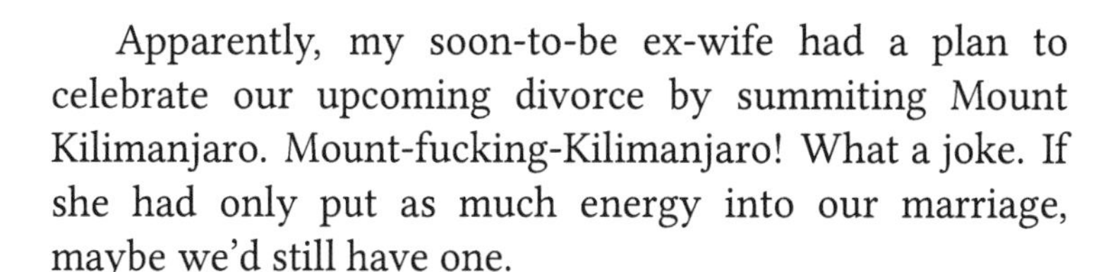

Apparently, my soon-to-be ex-wife had a plan to celebrate our upcoming divorce by summiting Mount Kilimanjaro. Mount-fucking-Kilimanjaro! What a joke. If she had only put as much energy into our marriage, maybe we'd still have one.

My celebration plan was to sell the house. Perhaps calling this a celebration was a stretch. Selling our home was a necessity, but deep down, I was glad to be done, both with the house and my overachiever wife.

This would be my second shattered marriage and I was just barely in my mid-thirties. My wife claimed "irreconcilable differences" as the reason for our divorce. Funny how in retrospect, it seemed our differences were irreconcilable from the day we met. It was just the way things were. I really didn't have a clue what she wanted from me. I thought what we had (our love) would be enough. Now, I'm not sure there was any love between us at all. Don't get me wrong, there was affection at times, and there was our lust, which sustained the relationship through the years. And to be honest, the sex was pretty good, right up to the end. We found a means to obtain pleasure in each other's arms, and this in many ways gave me hope. My wife, on the other hand, had a more pragmatic view of sex. She said I made her feel good. (A good thing, yes?) Then she went on to say, chocolate also made her feel good but she didn't need to be married to a Snickers Bar to enjoy it. She now calls me Baby Ruth.

I needed some advice. There was a trend being set that required undoing, some adjustment and although I seldom turned to, of all people, my mother for advice, I hoped she might provide some to her troubled son.

My mother began her "phoned in" advice by saying, "You know, I've always said, three strikes and you're out."

"What the hell is that supposed to mean?"

"What I'm saying, Son, is at a certain point you'll just have to sit yourself back down in the dugout."

"What's with the baseball analogies? Have you been bingeing on the Red Sox again? You know that only depresses you."

"Never mind about that. We're talking about you."

"Did I tell you she calls me Baby Ruth?"

"What? Why does she call you Babe Ruth?"

"No, Baby Ruth, after the candy bar."

"That's strange... Good candy bar, though. So why was it you called me again?"

I have no idea... "Mom, I called you for some parental advice. You remember what that is, right?"

"Don't be a smart-ass. My only advice to you is to step out of the batter's box, take a few practice swings before you continue, just relax a little. And don't chase curveballs."

"Is that what you did?"

"What...? Do you mean after I left your father? No, this lady retired, mid-career. In my prime, I turned in my bat and my glove."

"Well, I'm not sure I'm ready to retire my glove just yet." *I'm ready to end this ridiculous metaphor, though.* "Listen, you know me pretty well, right? So tell me straight. What am I doing wrong? I think I have to accept at least some of the blame."

There was silence on the line.

"Baby, you might be trying too hard. Whereas I... I tried too little."

"What do you mean tried too little? As I recall, you were the ideal wife. You were always so beautiful for him. The house was always so perfect."

"Yeah, I did keep a nice house back then, didn't I? But that's beside the point. What I'm saying is, I didn't spend enough time on me. I didn't take enough time trying to understand what I needed. What I wanted. I didn't have an idea who I was. And as a result, my marriage didn't have a soul or anything resembling a foundation. We were just cufflinks and high heels."

"So how is my trying too hard a shortcoming?"

"Because you're doing the same thing. Your father and I... Well, maybe I should speak for myself. Because I didn't have a clue. I went through the motions. I did what my girlfriends did. I followed the socialization guidebook given to me as a girl." She chuckled, "An instruction manual that taught me to fold my hands and keep quiet, to smile, to be nice, make friends and grow up one day to be a good wife. Somewhere along the way, it seems you found a similar book, but one devoted to love and relationships, and you became a devout follower, never stopping to ask what you thought about it. You swallowed every word hook, line and sinker."

"Yes... I see what you're saying. I gobbled it up, line and verse. I memorized the damn thing. It defined every move I made and I never questioned a word or asked myself why."

Mom's comment about the instruction manual brought me back to a conversation I had with a friend I served with in the Air Force. He'd criticized my devotion to the Aircraft Operator's Manual of my current jet. He was on the side of innovation and exploration of the limits of the aircraft, and I was on the side of complete and blind adherence to the rules, limitations and procedures described in it. I argued there was no place for personal input or interpretation. He said something then I have never forgotten. He asked, "Can it fly the thing? If so, just put the damn Operator's Manual on the pilot's seat and see what happens. Nothing. Right? It's you who flies the airplane."

"So take the rest of the season off," Mom said. "Go get yourself a good batting coach and work on that swing."

"Mom, you're starting to scare me. Quit with the baseball lingo."

"And make sure your coach brings a big mirror along."

"Why? To help me work on my stance?"

"No. To try to find yourself in it, Honey."

"Trying to find myself in it. Huh! You know, Old Lady, you're pretty good at this parental advice stuff after all. Thanks. Oh and by the way, you're not chewing tobacco again, are you?"

"Love ya, Son."

"Love you too, Mom."

I wonder how many games I've watched since that phone conversation? How many ball or strike calls I've gotten wrong? How many "errors" I've groaned at? How many runs I've cheered? Baseball is a vastly different game now. The "Curse of the Bambino" has finally lifted and the Red Sox won the World Series after an eighty-six-year drought. Mom would have been ecstatic.

For better and for worse, so much in my life has changed as well.

Now, the light of my Sun and Darkness are my only welcome companions. They are a hand to hold, a shoulder to cry on, and an ear for these reminiscences. Within

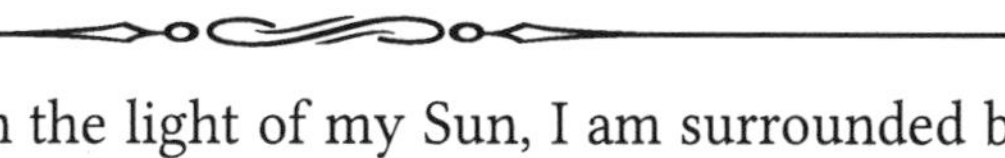

Darkness and in the light of my Sun, I am surrounded by the mechanisms of modern technology to help me to breathe, and others that confirm my dwindling existence.

Darkness has no voice, and for that I am grateful. I can sense its dismay when I fumble for the light button on my bedside to beckon the overhead light's return. Yet artificial light has little effect on me.

Darkness is patient, it allows for slow, quiet contemplation and insists on only truth. Artificial light, on the other hand, can be tricky and fast, pulling one's attention from one shiny surface or thought to another.

I still have a television. I don't spend as much time watching it as I once did. I use it as a way to distract from pain or as a measure of time. It takes about seven to ten minutes to search the fifteen channels. Stopping at each station to get an update on the weather, politics, sports, or to gain an appreciation of a new device, manufactured to correctly fold your underwear. I say the television is a measuring tool because when I am given pain medication, depending on what it is, it takes from one to two circuits through the channels before I feel relief.

My Sun doesn't rise at the same time every day. It sometimes rises after breakfast, in the afternoon, or sometimes, with equal parts of awe and regret, it rises to shine on my day at night.

My Sun rises to the familiar sound of footsteps approaching swiftly from down the hall. Her heels ring as church chimes, welcoming the new hour. As she peeks around the door, I first glimpse her blazing brightness, and I don't look away. She comes to me and kisses my face and thaws me with her embrace. I can smell the floral subtleness of perfume and her long silvery hair blankets my chest, enhancing her warming effect.

I whisper "Good morning" into her ear.

"It's two o'clock, Sweetie."

"I know."

She takes off her coat and drapes it over the back of the chair, settles in at my bedside. "So, how ya doing Babe, what kind of a day are you having?"

I hear the import of her question, understanding how the character of my answer will impact the path of the visit. If I give her a detailed back-brief of my unending discomfort, her focus will shift to the staff. Or on the other hand, if I gloss over my ills, she will continue her questioning and therefore be equally distracted by concerns with my well being. This was our dance.

"I had some pain earlier, but just recently, I've begun to feel much better." I look into her eyes to assess the effectiveness of my little lie.

"I see... Well, good!" She takes my hand, and her smile indicates she will follow my lead.

Her fingers are uncharacteristically cold in my hands.

"And how was church? Did you speak to anyone I like? Did the minister suggest another snappy dirge to be played at my funeral?" I rub her hands, attempting to bring back their heat.

She smiled again. "Everyone I spoke to asked about you and sends their love and concern."

"Their 'love and concern', how sweet."

"Some were sincere. At least, they seemed to be."

"Remember, they're well trained. Our friendly acquaintances have learned how to expertly feign empathy, how to politely express warmth where none truly exists."

"You're in a good mood today. What's wrong?"

"You know what's wrong."

She looks at me for a long time, takes a deep breath and whispers, "I love you."

Her words sweep over me like a flame; I listen to their clarity. At the appropriateness of their utterance, and the effect is astonishing. "You see, that's the problem."

"That I say, I love you, to my husband?"

"No, the problem is, you really do."

Ours was a long journey coming to this place. The mirror suggested by my mother over three decades ago, still holds a prominent place, demanding my gaze. And to good effect. The mirror has shown me the singularity of my being, my uniqueness. Not that I am special, just different. I needed a new set of rules to see, understand and authentically experience real love and affection. It was necessary to look into myself to find what was really important. And a funny thing happened: I realized I had to focus my awareness outwards, as well. To understand what love meant to others I cared for. How they defined it. This, too, had to be seen. This was not a place for presumption. Yes, I was free to guess, but often that was just folly.

I learned to listen. I learned to allow others to be themselves. And I came to see, that if in the end, they were not a person I could love, it was okay. Failing in love wasn't my fault and certainly not theirs. Yet through it all, along that rocky, uncertain way, I finally found her.

The serendipity of our meeting, I have often pondered. I wondered if the universe gave her to me as a commendation for my service in the Gulf War. *Probably not.* Or, as someone to fill the void left by the passing of my mother. Whatever the reason or cause, I am grateful to have recognized her light when it shone my way. Perhaps it was she who successfully illuminated the path for me.

"Yes, Sweetheart, it's true; I really do love you." She and I giggle at her rhyme. "Have you eaten lunch yet?"

I say, "I'm not hungry," and my expression darkens. "Look, I want to thank you for being here with me. For being with me through, well… this."

"There's no place I'd rather be." She retakes my hand, and her eyes beam as brightly as her words.

"I can think of a few."

She smiles, but it isn't a smile of delight. Then it's gone completely and she says, "What am I going to do without you? I don't want you to leave me."

Our conversations lately teeter like this, from light to dark. I didn't have an answer.

I imagine then, her as a much older woman, with gray, soil-stained work gloves, weeding in her garden under a cloud-shrouded sky. I can see her reading in her favorite chair, and lifting her chin to watch a flight of Snow Geese honk across the valley below. I imagine the thousands of mornings she will wake up without me by her side. I can see the calamity my death will be to her.

And my mind turns to heaven, to these questions: *If there is a heaven, will I be welcomed? Is my soul of sufficient virtue to be allowed to enter? Perhaps yes, perhaps no.* One side hoped for the latter. Maybe I didn't want to enter. *How can I wander in the splendor of heaven, for who knows how long—without her?* This is a perplexing paradox. I'd prefer oblivion.

How can heaven be a sanctuary of peace, with her still here on earth, alone? Is this hubris or benevolence born of a love beyond the confines of this world? I remain silent, contemplating this enigma, and I look at her. I peer into the eyes of the love of my life, into my Sun slowly setting, and think: Well, *I guess that's just another Wonder of the World.*

The End

for Dale, my Sun.

Last Thing on the List

Toni Kief

Toni Kief is from a small Midwestern town and a family of high spirits. Presently in the Pacific Northwest, she stays for the view, trees and friends. Her life story includes years in Insurance. A longtime civil rights activist, she shares stories about lunches with politicians, leaders and artists. Toni didn't start writing until she was sixty years old. She gathers stories prime for embellishments in unlikely situations. Toni has several works of fiction independently published and working on Historical fiction. She is a founding director of The Writers Cooperative of the Pacific Northwest.

Sometimes, love is smarter than we are. It doesn't just know what we want, it can procure it for us in unexpected ways. And it knows that when our goal is reached, there is always something new on the horizon.

Immediately after refilling the baggie with ice, Ed went back to his chair in the living room. Holding the bag against his face, Ed pulled out the worn piece of notebook paper from his wallet. He had carried this list since his teens. He studied it, and noticed how his writing had matured, and then aged. Today, a line goes through item number one; the first and the last.

This was the wish that started his search for adventure and dreams and became the design of his life. They call it a bucket list these days, but for Ed, these were his goals.

The discolored paper is frail and covered on both sides with numbers and scribbles. Much of the ink has faded, but number one stood clear. The page started before high school, and he visualized his hand when it printed number 1, but today it's over. Expecting a feeling of victory, Ed only found sadness as if this was the funeral of his oldest friend. He glanced at all of the other accomplishments. All completed.

He watched his now wrinkled hand pick up the ballpoint pen. There was a tear as he marked a line through number one, "Catch a foul ball at Wrigley Field." As a boy he was thought this would be easy, he had a glove, terrible seats, and the Cubs. How hard could it be? This was a sure recipe for success. As the years slipped away, he quit taking the glove, but he still went to every game. Last year, because of his health, Ed retired. At Renee's insistence, they moved to Arizona, to be near the kids. Ed rejected Scottsdale and compromised with Mesa so he could still go to spring training. She didn't argue. She had lived with his Cubs addiction since they met at the season opener in 1967.

He pushed the recliner back to the perfect position and flipped on Sports Center just as they ran the video. Completing his dream had gone viral. Even Ed laughed as he watched an elderly man stand up in the Arizona sun and reach out for the ball as it went screaming into the cheap seats. He stretched, and it touched his fingertips and then crashed into his face. A hot dog vendor snatched the ricocheted rocket and completed his own dream. Ed watched as he fell out of the stands and slumped onto the field. Even with the video, he still wasn't sure what happened. Today, he has a perfect imprint on the left cheek under the bag of ice. That was as good as a catch for Ed.

The biggest lesson Ed learned in a long life was to adapt. Almost nothing on the list ever manifested as he planned. The Cubs Organization gave him a new autographed ball and paid for his emergency medical. They insisted he take a check for $2,000. He explained he didn't want money, only the ball. Their attorney continued to lecture about liability and other legalese. Ed let them talk, and then signed with no hesitation. Before he left the meeting, however, Ed begged them not to fire the vendor; he understood how an errant hit is too tempting for the hopeful. They would never know that this was only about the game.

As he finished a quick doze in the chair, he noticed next to the crumpled list on his lap, a new piece of paper. With an all too familiar script was a list. The only number filled in was one—Paris Airshow—and the numbers continued down the page, begging for new dreams.

He glanced towards the noise in the kitchen, "Damn, I love that woman."

Acknowledgments

The Authors in this book would like to thank the other members of the Everett Creative Writers Group for their patience in putting up with our ranting, proselytizing and politicking even in our regular meetings, as we have no doubt done, and for still coming week after week anyway.

The Everett Creative Writers Group as a whole would like to thank the Vintage Café and Romio's Pizza for hosting us during this process, as well as Panera and Bob's Burgers and Brew for hosting us in the past.

We would also like to thank Elika Kohen, our wonderful layout-specialist-person for helping us turn all these loose words on electronic pages and in all different formats into an actual book.

The life of a writer can be very fulfilling, but living with one can be hard, so we would all like to thank our families and loved ones and especially our respective significant others for their tolerance and support in this endeavor.

Made in the USA
Middletown, DE
27 February 2019